PUDDLY THE PENGUIN

By Bryant Oden

©2013 Bryant Oden

Songdrops Press

PART ONE
LOST AND ALONE

Chapter 1
Penguin Valley

Puddly the Penguin was excitedly waddling across the snow to his papa on a crisp, cool morning in Penguin Valley. The sun was just starting to come up over one of the little hills surrounding the valley, and as Puddly often did, he stopped for a moment, closed his eyes, and felt the warm sunshine on his face. "Awwwe, one of my very favorite things," he said. "I bet the sun likes it too. It must like warming up penguin faces or it wouldn't do it so good."

Then he started waddling again. It took him longer than most penguins his age, because he was smaller than most penguins his age. Sometimes he didn't mind that too much. Other times, he really did.

"Come on, feet. Almost there!"

When he reached his papa, he said "Mamma told me you're taking another fishing group to the ocean!"

"That's right, Puddly," his papa said. "We've been waiting for days to make sure the Night Winds won't be too bad to spend the night there, but we can't wait any more. We're almost out of fish."

"Can I go this time, Papa? I'm old enough now! I'm days and days and DAYS older since the last time you went!"

"I'm sorry, Puddly. Not yet. But before too much longer, it will be the warm season, and we'll all go to the ocean together and stay there until it's winter again."

"But Papa, I don't want to wait any longer! Fuzzly and Nightsong got to go when they were my age! It's only fair you let me go too!"

"I know it doesn't feel good, Puddly. But you're a little smaller than they were at your age, and it takes a half day of moving fast to get there. And this time of year the Night Winds can be extra cold and windy. Especially near the ocean. That's why we can't live there in the winter. And sometimes the wind makes a lot of blowing snow, and that can build up and make it a lot harder to waddle. Especially for a younger penguin."

"But Papa, I AM big enough to go! I'm a lot bigger than I was when I was a lot smaller than I am! It's not fair!" Puddly stomped his foot on a small patch of slippery ice, lost his balance, and fell on his back side. He got up as fast as he could and said "I AM big enough, Papa! I really am!"

"I know you don't like my decision, Puddly, but it's to keep you safe and to make sure the ten of us bring back all the fish we can for all the penguins in the valley. If I said you could go, you might feel happy for now, but that wouldn't be taking good care of you. It can be rough out there for a little guy."

"I'm NOT that little! And I can't help my size! It's not fair!"

"Sometimes life doesn't feel fair, Puddly. You'll get to go to the ocean before too long, sure as snow."

"But Papa, I want to go THIS time! THEY got to! IT'S NOT FAIR!"

"Puddly Sunfacer Furfoot, that's enough! You can spend the rest of the day being mad and miserable, or you can accept it, feel sad for a while, and move on with a pretty good day. That's your choice. But either way, this decision is what seems best to me, and it's final."

"You're mean! I don't like you!" Puddly waddled off as fast as he could to be alone on his favorite little hill.

"No sense going after him when we're both feeling a little frustrated," his papa thought. "I'll have a good talk with him after I get back home tomorrow, when we're both feeling more relaxed." He took a big breath of fresh, cool air, let it go, and headed off to round up the other penguins in the fishing group.

Chapter 2
Splashers the Dolphin

"One day, one day soon, I'm going to swim back home," thought young Splashers the dolphin, just like he had thought a hundred times before. "As soon as the weather is good and the ocean is calm and all the conditions are just right, I'm going to start the Big Swim. It's going to take me a lot of days, maybe even a whole season or more, but I'll do it. And then I'll finally be back in those sunny, beautiful blue green waters, with my mamma and brother and all my friends. I'll finally be home again."

Splashers picked up speed, jumped into the air, sailed over a small iceberg, and landed gracefully back in the icy water.

He smiled as he thought of all the other dolphins seeing him swimming towards them. "Is that— Is that Splashers?" Poptail would say. "Could it really be him? Mamma! It's Splashers! He's back! Hey everyone, Splashers is back!"

And they would all swim up to him as fast as they could, and his mamma would be so happy to see her long lost Splashers she would cry. And Poptail would circle around him a few times, and everyone would be so excited. And then his mamma would say "Splashers, where have you been for so long? What happened? We thought... we thought we had lost you forever!"

And he would wait for them all to gather around, and then he would tell them his story. "They really won't believe it," he thought. "And as for me, I won't have to be alone anymore in this cold, strange, empty world, far away from where I belong. I'll finally be back home."

Chapter 3
Sunshine Hill

"It's not fair! It's just not fair! Papa doesn't care about me or he would let me go!" said Puddly, as he waddled towards his favorite place in the whole world, Sunshine Hill. He started zigzagging up the hill the way his papa had taught him. "Papa says trying to waddle straight up an icy hill is the fastest way to find yourself upside down at the bottom of it!"

When Puddly reached the top, he looked back at the little valley where all the penguins lived during the harsh winter months. It was like a big shallow bowl, with little hills circling all around it that helped block the wind, making Penguin Valley the best place to be on cold, windy nights. From down there you couldn't see past all the little hills. But up on Sunshine Hill, Puddly felt like he was on the top of the world. He could see the whole valley. And when he turned around, he could see far into the endless Great Open, all the way to Sea Way Hill, where his papa's fishing group would be heading on their way to the ocean. He looked back at little Penguin Valley, and watched all the penguins doing their penguiny things. Some were bustling around, some were standing and talking, and some, mostly younger ones, were on the other side of the valley, sliding down Cold Butt Hill. Then he spotted his papa, looking small and far away, talking with a couple of the penguins who would be going with him on the fishing trip.

"Why won't you let me go, Papa?" He said quietly. "I AM big enough! It's not fair! It's not my fault I'm kind of small! I feel like you're punishing me for something I can't help! And on the inside I'm as big as any penguin! I am! I'm really smart, and I'm pretty brave when there's nothing too scary around, and I work really hard when you or Mamma make me. I know I really AM big enough! But you won't even give me a chance to prove it! I know I can make it all the way to the ocean and help you catch fish for everyone! I could even make it there alone! I could! Sure as snow! I could even beat you there! I could get there faster than all of you, and catch a bunch of big fish before you even get there! The biggest fish you ever saw! Then when you slowbirds finally show up, I'll say 'What took you so long? Is this enough fish for you?' And I'll show you the biggest pile of the biggest fish you've ever seen! That will show you! And maybe you'll be mad for a blink or two, Papa. But when you see all the fish I caught, and when you see how all the other penguins are so amazed, then you'll just be happy and proud of me! And then you'll even let me lead the whole fishing group back home! IF they can keep up! And they'll all sing a waddle song about Puddly the Great Fish-Catching Penguin! And when we get home, I'll be a hero, and no one will ever call me little again! Nobody! Not big enough to go? We'll see about that! I'll show you, Papa. I'll show you!"

And before Puddly had even stopped to think about what he was doing and whether it was really a very good idea, his small penguin feet had started to waddle down the other side of Sunshine Hill, towards the Great Open, on their way to Sea Way Hill and the ocean. "I'll show you, Papa! I'll show everyone!"

Chapter 4
The Big Swim

Splashers rolled over on his back and let his belly feel the warm morning sun, as he thought about how excited everyone would be to see him again, and how eager they would be to hear what happened. "Tell us your story, Splashers! Where in the world have you been all this time?"

And after all the dolphins gathered around to listen, Splashers would tell them about the day he was exploring the beautiful coral reef, like he often did, when he suddenly found himself tangled in a big fishing net. It closed around him, and he couldn't get free or come up for air. He struggled and struggled, holding his breath longer than he ever had before, but the ropes were too strong. He needed air desperately, and started to think he wasn't going to make it. But just when he was sure he couldn't hold his breath any longer, the net came up out of the water and he could breathe again.

And then he would tell them how there was a big boat, and how land people pulled the net onto it and put him in a small space, barely bigger than him. And how he got the feeling they never planned to let him swim free in the ocean again. And how he was there for days and days, and each day was a little colder. But then one day there was a big storm, and the boat was starting to rock back and forth from the waves. And suddenly, a big wave tipped the boat over on its side and he was free. But in strange, cold, icy waters, far from home.

"And then I'll tell them about my Big Swim all the way back home, that I'm going to start any day now," he thought. "Just as soon as all the conditions are really right."

Splashers gathered speed to jump over another small iceberg. He jumped up high into the air, sailed over it, and slapped his tail against the water as he landed, to make an extra loud splash. "It will be so good to see everyone again. So good to see Mamma and Poptail and all my friends. So good to be back in those warm, beautiful blue-green waters. Back where I belong. But it will take a long, long time to swim all that way. Through new waters I've never swam in before. And I need to wait for just the right time. But one day, one day soon, I'm going to start the Big Swim back home."

Chapter 5
Clear as Ice

It only took a few steps down the other side of Sunshine Hill for Puddly to be somewhere he had never been before. "Stay where we can see you," his mamma always said. "You can go to the top of your little hill, Puddly, but never down the other side, out of view. Understand?"

"Clear as ice, Mamma. I understand."

He stopped a moment, and took a last look at Penguin Valley. "I'm sorry, Mamma," he said quietly. "But I have to show Papa that I AM big enough to go on his trip. I know you'll be mad when you find out what I did, but when we get back and you hear how I caught so many big fish, you'll see why I did it. And then you'll be proud of me like Papa will be. Don't worry about me, Mamma. I'll be extra, extra carefu— WHOA!"

Just then, Puddly slipped, fell down, and started sliding down the far side of Sunshine Hill. It wasn't too steep, and after being scared for a few fast heart beats, he started to enjoy it. "Woooohoooooooo!"

When he reached the bottom of the hill, he got up and looked around. He was used to seeing the Great Open, with its endless snow and ice and gentle hills. And he was used to seeing Sea Way Hill off in the distance straight ahead, and the far away white mountains off to the side. But as he looked all around, he realized this was the very first time that he couldn't see another penguin anywhere. He wasn't used to that at all. For the first time in his life, Puddly was really alone.

As he stood there, looking at the vast open space in front of him, he felt a sudden wave of fear in his stomach. He tried to talk himself into feeling better.

"It's okay to feel a little scared, Puddly. Of course you do. This is the first time you've ever not been able to see other penguins nearby. The first time you're leaving Penguin Valley. The first time you're having your very own adventure."

He closed his eyes, faced the morning sun, and relaxed just a little. As he did, he had another feeling inside. A kind of feeling that was clear as ice, but quiet enough he could ignore it if he wanted to, that maybe this wasn't the best idea he ever had. In fact, it was probably the worst idea he ever had. Yup, it was definitely the worst idea he ever had, and he should just turn around right now and zigzag right back up Sunshine Hill before his mamma notices she can't see him anywhere. That would be the smart thing to do.

"Papa really just wanted to keep me safe. He wasn't trying to be mean. He loves me, and he does the best he can to take care of me and everything else he has to take care of, even if I don't like what he says sometimes. I should just turn around right now and go back. But the thing is, he was wrong. I AM big enough to go. I really am! But he just wouldn't believe me! 'You're not big enough yet, Puddly!' Well, we'll see about that, won't we? I'm gonna show him! I'm gonna catch the biggest pile of the biggest fish ever! Sure as snow!"

And before Puddly had really realized what happened, he had pushed away the little feeling in him that knew it would be a very good idea to turn around, and he was putting his whole heart into being upset again.

"I'm TIRED of everyone saying I'm too little to do things! I'm TIRED of it! And if I go home now, they'll just keep saying it! If I turn around, I won't get to beat the fishing group to the ocean and catch a bunch of big fish and be the hero and show everyone how big I really am! So let's get moving, feet! No one is gonna stop me from doing this! Not even me! Watch out, fish! Here I come!"

Chapter 6
Soon

Splashers swam full speed towards a small, flat iceberg, and got ready to jump. "You can do it. Steady. Steady."

When he had almost reached it, he jumped up high into the air and did a double spin. That was when he saw that the iceberg was longer than he had expected, and there was no way he was going to be able to jump all the way over it. "Uh oh. I think this is going to be a rough landing!" He came down right on the iceberg and slid forward all the way into the water. SPLASH!

"Hey, that was fun! I might be the first dolphin ever to go ice sliding! But I wish I could show Mamma and Poptail. Fun is more fun when you can share it with someone."

He jumped up out of the water again, did a flip, and splashed back down into the cold.

"Don't worry, Mamma. I'm okay, and I'll be home before too long. It's just a really, really long swim. The boat was moving a whole lot faster than I can and it still took a long time to get here. And I just don't quite feel ready yet. I'm just waiting for the right day. For the ocean currents and the weather and everything to all feel right. But soon I'll start the Big Swim, and one day you'll see me swimming up to you, and it will be one of the happiest days ever. Soon, Mamma. You'll see. Soon."

But deep down, Splashers was starting to wonder if he would ever start the Big Swim at all.

Chapter 7
Sea Way Hill

Puddly kept waddling forward into the Great Open, slowly getting closer to Sea Way Hill. It was taking longer than he had expected, but it was pretty easy going. The ground was mostly flat and hard and snow-packed, with little patches of slippery ice here and there, and a few little snow drifts now and then. But there weren't any big hills to climb and there wasn't any deep snow to waddle through. His adventure was starting out as easy as he had hoped. "I really can do this! I really am gonna go all the way to the ocean and catch a bunch of big big fish! Papa will be so surprised and proud, and then he'll tell me he was wrong, and I'll say 'That's okay, Papa. One day I'll probably be wrong about something too.' And everyone will be so amazed by what I did. It's gonna be great!"

Puddly decided to try to make up a little waddle song about how great it was going to be. He liked waddle songs because they were so easy to sing. You just had to speak them really loud and strong, in rhythm to your feet. But he had never tried to make one up before. "Here I go. My very first waddle song!

"It's gonna be great!
It's gonna be great!
It's gonna be great!
It's gonna be great!"

He was having a little trouble thinking of more words.

"It's gonna be great!
It's gonna be great!
It's! Gonna! Be!
Great! Great! GREAT!

"Well, not too bad for my very first waddle song. I wonder what I should call it."

Sea Way Hill was slowly getting bigger in front of him. And when he looked back, Sunshine Hill was slowly getting smaller. It made his stomach feel a little funny each time he looked back and saw that his home was a little farther away than the last time he looked.

"But I'm not gonna turn around! Nope! I'm gonna waddle all the way to the ocean, dive into the water and catch the biggest fish any penguin has ever caught! Easy Sneezy! I'm gonna show everyone! And then no one will say I'm little ever ever again!"

He kept plodding along, even though his legs were starting to get a little tired and a cold wind was starting to blow against his face. He didn't let himself stop and rest until it looked like he was about halfway to Sea Way Hill. And even then, he just stopped long enough to catch his breath. "Okay, feet, time to get moving again. Wow, Sea Way Hill really is getting bigger and closer!" He glanced behind him and his stomach felt funny again. "And Sunshine Hill really is getting smaller and farther."

More waddles later than he had hoped, Puddly finally reached the front of Sea Way Hill. "That turned out to be a longer walk than I thought! But I made it! Good job, feet!"

He waddled around the side of Sea Way Hill, eager to see what things looked like from the back of it. "Maybe the ocean will be right here! Maybe I've already made it!" But when he reached the back, his heart sank. "Yuckle doodle!"

Instead of seeing the ocean right in front of him, or even way in front of him, there was just more of the Great Open, everywhere he looked.

"I can't see the ocean anywhere! This isn't going the way I planned it at all! Then again, I didn't really plan it did I? My feet just started waddling. I don't think they really thought this whole thing through too good."

Puddly stood there looking at the endless snow and ice in front of him. "Now what do I do? I can't just keep waddling and hope I'm heading towards the ocean. I might get lost, and the Night Winds are too bad out here in the Great Open for a penguin to spend a night alone. But I don't want to just stand here until the fishing group sees me either. 'Oh, hi Papa. What took you all so long? Well, let's get moving!' That probably wouldn't work out so great. But what else can I do?"

Puddly was so focused on trying to figure things out that he didn't notice the air was getting colder and the wind was getting stronger. He just stood there, at the back of Sea Way Hill, looking at the endless icy world in front of him, feeling a little scared, a little tired, a little discouraged, and a lot unsure what to do.

Chapter 8
Very Much Alone

Splashers swam down into the water, and then darted up towards the surface, right in front of a small floating chunk of ice. Just as he was lifting up out of the water, he flipped his tail and slapped the ice into the air in front of him. Then he shot up high above the water and caught it with his mouth.

"Four times in a row. A new record! This is one thing I will miss a little. Ice games. We don't have any ice back home. But it did snow a little that one day. We all kept jumping up out of the water to catch snow drops. And once, Poptail and I weren't paying enough attention and we both jumped up into the air at the same time and bumped right into each other! That was such a fun day. But every day I spend here, in this cold, strange place, that day, and every day I was ever home, gets longer and longer ago."

Sometimes Splashers could picture home almost as clearly as being there. But other times, like now, he couldn't quite remember what it felt like to be in warm, blue-green waters, with the hot sun basking down on him, playing with Poptail in their favorite little cove, or playing Keep the Shell Away with the sea otters, until his mamma would call them home for the night. "I miss the cove. I miss the warmth. I miss Poptail. I miss Mamma. I miss home." Splashers looked around, at the ice lands not far from him, at the endless icy water everywhere else, and at the cold gray sky. And he felt very much alone.

Chapter 9
A Feeling Whisper

As Puddly stood there at the back of Sea Way Hill, looking at the vast Great Open as far as he could see, a quiet feeling began whispering deep inside him, that the best thing to do was to wait right there for the fishing group, waddle up to his papa and tell him exactly what happened. But he didn't like that idea very much at all. And since the feeling whisper wasn't very loud or demanding, he could easily cover it over by imagining catching the biggest fish ever. "It's gonna be great, great, great! Papa will be so amazed!" He just couldn't quite figure out how he could still make his big plan happen.

Then he got an idea. "I know what I'll do! I'll wait here and listen for them, and as soon as I hear which side of Sea Way Hill they're coming around, I'll waddle really fast around the other side so they never see me! Then I'll let them waddle on ahead of me a little, and I'll just follow behind them all the way to the ocean! That means I won't get to be there waiting for them with a big pile of fish, but when I do get there, they'll all be so impressed that I came all that way, they'll see that I really was big enough after all! And then I can still catch the biggest fish they've ever, ever seen! I just have to learn how to swim first. And how to catch fish. But right after that, I'll catch the biggest fish EVER! Sure as snow! And then Papa will see, they'll all see, how big I really am!"

So Puddly, relieved that he had a plan, started listening for the fishing group so he could make sure he had time to get far enough around the opposite side of Sea Way Hill to hide. "I was waddling really fast so they probably won't be here for a long time. But Papa always says it's better to be ready than snoozy." Just then, he started to hear the faint sounds of penguins coming around the same side of Sea Way Hill that he had taken.

"Wow, they got here pretty fast! They must have really been hurrying! Okay, feet. Let's get moving!"

As Puddly started waddling around the other side of Sea Way Hill, back towards the front, he heard a distant laugh that he knew was his papa's. Puddly always loved that laugh. A lot of times his papa was a little bit serious, a little bit busy, a little bit tired, or a little bit grumpy. But when he would laugh, his eyes would shine and his smile would spread to all the penguins around him. And that always made Puddly feel happy, and made his papa seem like the safest place in the whole world.

But this time it made Puddly feel kind of nervous to hear his papa, waddling with the fishing group just on the other side of the hill.

"If Papa knew I was right here, out in the middle of nowhere, just a quick waddle from where he is, wow, he would really, I mean he would really, really…, well actually, I don't know what the blizzard he would do! He'd be shocked and surprised and mad and glad I was safe and I don't know what else, all at once. But I do know I would be in big, big trouble, and he would probably ask someone from the fishing group to walk me all the way back home. Yuckle doodle!"

Puddly kept waddling towards the front of Sea Way Hill to make sure no one saw him. As the sounds of the fishing group disappeared, that feeling whisper inside Puddly came up again. It wasn't an angry feeling, or a bossy feeling, or a judging feeling, or an upset feeling. It was just a quiet, kind, simple, matter of fact "Puddly, you already know in your heart what you should do" kind of feeling. And this time, maybe because after so much waddling he was feeling a little too tired to push it away again, or maybe because he just knew inside that the feeling whisper was good to listen to, he let himself notice it more. For the first time, he let himself really hear it.

"Puddly, you know it wasn't really a good idea to leave home. You knew it even during your first few steps. You pushed it away and ignored it, but you always knew it. And right now, you know the best thing you can do is waddle right up to the fishing group, so Papa knows you're out here in the middle of nowhere, and tell him that you know you messed up, and you're really sorry. Yes, you will be in trouble. But you're far from home in the middle of the Great Open. No one knows where you are, and the most important thing is that you get safe. Being in trouble with your mamma and papa, who love you, is nothing compared to actually being unsafe, lost and alone. That's what real trouble is. And remember how Papa says, it never, ever works to run away from facing something you know you'll have to face sooner or later. The longer you wait to face something you're dreading, the bigger it gets."

As Puddly reached the front of Sea Way Hill, far out of sight of his papa and the fishing group, who were probably just now reaching the back, he could see Sunshine Hill, far off in the distance in front of him. "Wow, I sure am far away from home. And nobody even knows it!"

Puddly knew the feeling whisper in him was right, even though it felt scary to even consider it. As he pictured himself going around again to the back of Sea Way Hill to his papa, he felt a big cloud of dread. "If I do that, I'll be in such big trouble. Bigger trouble than I've ever, ever been in. And whoever has to walk me home won't be happy about it at all. And then that's one less penguin to catch fish, and everyone in the valley will hear about it and be mad at me.

I'll be in the worst trouble ever! Yuckle doodle! I've messed up so bad!"

But it was still ice crystal clear to him, the best thing he could do now was go catch up with the fishing group and tell his papa everything. He felt a sudden ripple of fear in his stomach as he pictured waddling up to his papa. He wasn't sure he was brave enough to go through with it. He thought of something his mamma sometimes said to him when he was scared. "It's okay to feel scared sometimes, Puddly. Everyone does. Being brave, having a courageous heart, doesn't mean you don't ever feel scared. It means even if it really scares you, even if it scares you more than anything ever has, you still do what you know in your heart is good to do. That's what real courage is, Puddly."

"Am I brave, Mamma?" he had asked her once.

"We don't know how much courage we have until we have a chance to be courageous. But I know you have a courageous heart inside you, Puddly. You just have to let it lead the way when it asks you to follow it."

As Puddly looked at Sunshine Hill, so far away, his heart pounded in his chest. "Well I guess this is my first real chance to show I have a courageous heart. I'm gonna be in such big trouble! But I do know this is what's best to do. I'm sure of that. Being brave doesn't mean you aren't scared. It means you do what you know is good to do, even if you really really are."

Chapter 10
Deep Down

Splashers darted down deep into the water, blew a big air bubble, and then watched it wobble upwards while he counted to five. Then he swam up towards it at full speed, touched it with his nose just before it reached the surface, and shot out of the water high into the air. "Barely made it," he thought, as he splashed back down. "Now I'll count to six and see if I can still make it in time. I have to get in really good shape before I can start the Big Swim."

But it was getting harder and harder for Splashers to believe he was really doing anything at all, except avoiding the one thing he knew deep down he needed to do. Start the Big Swim back home.

Chapter 11
Tear Sickles

Puddly took one last look at Sunshine Hill off in the distance, and then told his feet to turn around and start waddling towards his Papa. But they didn't listen. He told them again, but they still didn't move. He took a big breath of cool air and shook himself out of just standing there. "Come on, feet! You got me into this mess, you get me out! Let's get moving!" This time he was off and waddling, back around Sea Way Hill to catch up with the fishing group. "Papa! Papa!" he shouted. "Wait! It's me! I really messed up and I'm really, really sorry and I know I'm in big big trouble, but I just want to get all this over with. I just want to be with you and Mamma and Nightsong and even Fuzzly again! Papa, wait! PAPA!"

He kept calling for his papa as loud as he could, as he waddled around towards the back of Sea Way Hill. He stopped a couple of times, just long enough to listen for the fishing group, but couldn't hear them. "Papa! Wait for me! Please WAIT!"

When he reached the back of Sea Way Hill, tired and out of breath, he saw the fishing group in front of him, a lot farther ahead than he had imagined they could possibly be. Were they even too far away to hear him? He waddled after them at full speed. "Papa! Papa! Wait! It's me! I'm here! I messed up really bad and left on my own and I'm really really sorry! Papa! Wait! PAPA!"

He was getting a little closer to them, but was so tired and out of breath he just couldn't waddle anymore. He had to stop. He called to them as loud as he possibly could. "PAPA! WAIT! HELP! I'm back HERE! Please turn around! It's me! PAPA!"

But the fishing group never stopped or turned around. It was then that Puddly realized the wind was a lot stronger than it had been earlier, especially here at the back side of Sea Way Hill. It was blowing right towards him, muffling his voice from reaching the fishing group, which was now quickly getting farther and farther away.

"They can't hear me and I can't catch up to them! Yuckle doodle!" Puddly started jumping up and down and waving frantically. He took in the biggest breath he could and shouted one last time, with all his strength. "PAPA! WAIT! I'M BACK HERE! SOMEBODY!" But the fishing group just kept getting farther away. "They must be moving extra fast because of the wind getting stronger." He kept waving towards them as he tried to catch his breath. "Please look back, Papa. Please look back, anybody!" But no one did.

To make things worse, ground clouds of blowing snow were rising up across the Great Open in front of him, making it harder for him to see the fishing group. And in no time, he had lost sight of them completely.

"Now they can't hear me OR see me! I'm all alone again. I can't believe the big mess I got myself into! I never knew I could ever make a mess this big! I can't even do the right thing right! Now what the blizzard am I gonna do? Double yuckle doodle!"

Puddly was cold and tired, and the winter sun was already starting to get a little lower. "I don't really care about getting in trouble any more. I just have to make sure I don't spend a long night alone in the Great Open! Especially with the Night Winds as cold and strong as it looks like they're gonna be tonight!"

Puddly knew he couldn't just stand there. He either had to try to follow the fishing group to the ocean or turn around and head back home to Penguin Valley. He needed to make a decision fast and get moving. Surely the ocean wasn't too much farther. Surely it was a shorter walk than waddling all the way back home all by himself. Besides, with the blowing snow making it hard to see very far, he wasn't even sure he would be able to see Sunshine Hill to know he was going the right way. Then he might not make it home before dark. And one of the first things every penguin learns is that during the Night Winds, penguins who don't make it home before dark might not make it home at all.

It felt a little safer and more comforting to think of following after his papa than trying to make it all the way back to Penguin Valley all alone. It felt better knowing his papa was somewhere in front of him, not too far away, even if he couldn't see the fishing group and no one in the world knew where he was. And the ocean just couldn't be too much farther. It just couldn't be. Puddly had made up his mind. "Okay, feet. Let's get waddling! And no funny stuff this time!" He started waddling full speed after the fishing group.

Puddly half-heartedly called for his papa a few more times, but he knew that with the harsh wind they weren't close enough to hear him. Then he said, so quietly he could barely hear it himself, "Papa, please don't leave me here all alone. Please come back and get me. I'm really sorry I waddled off on my own. I'm really really sorry. Please, Papa. Please?"

He had no idea if his papa was already way far ahead or just kind of far ahead. He looked around to see if there were any penguin tracks, but the fierce wind was blowing away even his own tracks almost as fast as he was making them. Sometimes he noticed his tired feet had slowed down a lot, and then he would tell them to speed up again. "I can't leave my feet alone even for a blink or they just start doing whatever they want! Sometimes they just don't listen to me at all!"

As Puddly plodded along, he was getting more and more tired, and the strong wind blowing straight towards him made each step even harder. There wasn't any sign of the fishing group or the ocean. Just more and more ground clouds of blowing snow.

He finally let himself stop to rest his tired legs. He turned towards the low afternoon sun and closed his eyes. But as soon as he did, a small gray cloud covered it, and he was all alone. "Awwwe, please come back, sun. It would feel a lot better to know you're still with me." He tried to comfort himself with a little poem his mamma sometimes said to him at sleep time.

"When the strong wind blows
The sun's still there
When the warm day goes
The sun's still there
When the storm clouds come
The sun's still there
When the day is done
The sun's still there

You can't see it
You can't feel it
But in your heart
You can know it

And if you wait another day
You'll see it shine and chase away
All the dark and all the gray
And then you'll smile, and you'll say
As you watch its grand display
And feel its first morning ray
It didn't really leave or stray
The sun was always there!"

His mamma's poems always made him feel better. But this time it just didn't seem to help much. He was starting to feel more scared. "I just really don't know if I can do this. I just really don't know if I can waddle much more. I just really don't know if I'm gonna be okay. The wind is getting stronger and colder and I'm getting more lost and alone and I can't see my papa or the fishing group anywhere. There's no sign of the ocean and my legs are getting tired and with all the blowing snow I just can't see very far in front of me at all! I just really don't know if I'm gonna find my papa before the Night Winds come. I just really really don't!"

Tears started forming in Puddly's eyes, quickly turning into little tear sickles on his cheeks. He wanted to just give up, plop down on the ice, and feel sorry for himself. But the sun would be going down for the night before very much longer. He had to keep moving.

"Let's go, Puddly," he sniffled. "The only thing to do now is to keep going until you reach the ocean, and hope you find the fishing group there. Come on, feet. You can do it."

Puddly started waddling again, slower than before. He was scared, sad, tired and the most alone he had ever been.

Chapter 12
Spinning in Circles

Splashers watched the low sun disappear behind a small gray cloud. "Here comes another long, cold, lonely night. But it's not here yet!" He started circling around a flat, round iceberg, not much bigger than him. He circled faster and faster, until the iceberg started to slowly spin in the same direction. Then he swam away from it, darted straight towards it, carefully jumped up onto it, and slid off the other side.

"One more try!" He circled it a few more times to get it spinning faster, swam away, headed straight towards it more slowly this time, jumped up a little, gently landed in the middle of the iceberg, and let it slowly spin him around in a circle. As he watched the world slowly move past him, his thoughts turned to the Big Swim, and how good it would feel to finally be back home. "Soon, Mamma. Maybe soon."

Chapter 13
The Circle of the Sun

Puddly, as cold and tired as he was, kept waddling forward in as straight a line as he could. "Come on, feet. We can do this. We just gotta keep waddling!"

The cloud-covered sun was getting lower, the wind was getting stronger, the air was getting colder, the blowing snow was getting snowier and Puddly was getting tireder.

As he kept plodding along, one heavy step at a time, he started thinking again about how worried his mamma must be back in Penguin Valley. She and the other penguins would have looked all over the valley for him by now. And with the wind already so cold and strong out in the Great Open, they couldn't do anything now but wait and worry and hope. "What have I done?" he sniffled. "I'm so sorry, Mamma. I'm just really so sorry."

Sometimes Puddly turned around and waddled backwards, so the bitter cold wind wasn't blowing on his face. It gave his tired legs a little bit of a break too. But it made it harder to know where he was going, and he fell down three different times. The third time, Puddly was so tired that instead of getting right back up, he let himself just lie there a while, looking up at the sky. It felt so good to just be plopped down on the ground instead of fighting the bitter wind with each heavy step. He started to think about how nice it would be to just stay plopped down and take a little nap. To just fall asleep a while, and drift off into a relaxed, safe, peaceful dream. Where he could get away from the biggest mess he'd ever gotten himself into. Wouldn't it be so nice to just fall asleep, and dream that he was safe and warm and cozy, with his mamma and papa, back home in Penguin Valley. He thought of sleep time the night before, which felt like forever ago, when his papa sang him a waddle song the fishing group sometimes sang on their trips to the ocean.

Steady and strong
We waddle along
Step after step

Singing this song
We won't give up
And we won't turn around
And we'll get back up
If we ever fall down
And sooner or later
Sure as the sun
We'll get where we're going
And then we'll be done!

"I love when Papa tells me sleep time stories or sings waddle songs," Puddly said as he relaxed in the snow. "I love sleep time. It's so nice to get all warm and cozy and just close my eyes and let myself sleeeeeeeep. It would feel so good right now, to just be done with this whole mess. To just be home, all safe and snug, and to just really sleeeeeeeeeeeeep."

Suddenly, Puddly realized he was drifting off. "Puddly Sunfacer Furfoot! You can NOT fall asleep out here in the middle of nowhere! It will be getting dark before long! I know you're tireder than you've ever ever been, but you have to get up! You have to start waddling again right now, Puddly! You just have to!"

Sometimes, Puddly tried not to feel scared. But right now, he was trying to scare himself enough to get a new burst of energy into his cold, tired body, and get back to waddling as fast as he could, as though his safety depended on it. Because it did.

He got back up, and started waddling again. "You can do it, Puddly! Just keep waddling! Steady and strong!" He started singing *Steady and Strong*, with as much energy as he could, making himself take two heavy, tired steps with every line.

> *"Steady and strong*
> *I waddle along*
> *Step after step*
> *Singing this song*
> *I won't give up*
> *And I won't turn around*
> *And I'll get back up*
> *If I ever fall down*
> *And sooner or later*
> *Sure as the sun*
> *I'll get where I'm going*
> *And then I'll be done!*

"Come on feet! You can do it! Steady and strong! Steady and strong!"

The bitter cold wind was blowing so hard now that Puddly had to lean forward as he waddled. And the blowing snow was so bad he could hardly see'in front of him at all. Each step was taking more effort than he had ever used in his life. He wondered how many more steps he would have to take to get to the ocean. "Do I have it in me to go a hundred more steps? Even more than that? I'm so tired and cold and scared, I just don't know if I can do it. I just really don't." He tried to imagine what his papa would say to help him.

"Just one step, Puddly. Just one. You don't have to take a hundred more steps right now. You just have to take one. Just this next step. That's all you ever have to do at any moment, Puddly. Just this next step. Just this next step."

Puddly started to feel a little more like maybe he could do it. He knew he could take just this next step. Then this next step.

"This step is for Mamma. I love you, Mamma. And I'm really, really sorry. You must be so worried right now. And this step is for Papa. Papa, I know you were just trying to keep me safe and make sure you caught enough fish. I'm really sorry I messed up so bad. And this step is for Nightsong. I might not ever say it to your face, but you're the best big sister a penguin could have, even if you do annoy me almost as much as I annoy you. And this step is for Fuzzly. I know we fight a lot, Fuzzly. But we have a lot of fun too. And to tell you the truth, I'd rather fight with you half the time than not have you around at all. I'm really glad all of you are my family. And if I get the chance, I promise I'll tell you that."

Puddly couldn't think of anyone else to take steps for. "Too bad I don't have a bigger family."

He looked over towards the setting sun, still hidden behind the same small cloud. "How can it be so windy but that one little cloud is just staying there hiding the sun from me? Selfish cloud!" He could tell that behind it, the sun was about to go down for the night.

He stopped waddling to rest his tired legs, and turned to face the cloud-covered sun. "I wish the sun would shine on me for just one little moment before it goes away. Just for a blink or two. Then I wouldn't feel so cold and scared and alone. Then I would know everything's gonna be okay. Then I would know the sun is with me.

"Please, sun. Please shine on my face one last time before the night chases you away. Little cloud, please move over just a little, so I can feel the last few rays of the sun. Icy wind, please blow that stubborn gray cloud out of the way. Please let me feel the sun one last time before it's gone. Please show me I'm not all alone, and that somehow I'm gonna be okay tonight. Please?"

Puddly stood there, watching hopefully. But the cloud didn't move. And the setting sun didn't break through the cloud to shine its last rays of the day on his cold face.

Little tear sickles formed on Puddly's cheeks again. "No last rays of sunshine. No promise that everything is gonna be okay. No help anywhere at all. I guess I really am all alone. Goodbye, sun. See you tomorrow." But he wasn't at all sure he would.

As he watched the cloud-covered sun slowly set behind the far away mountains, he remembered his mamma saying, one dark and cold night, "We can't have the sun all to ourselves, Puddly.

If we did, other penguins somewhere else would never get to feel it. But we can remember it, and know in our hearts that it's still shining, just as bright as ever."

"But it looks and feels like it's gone, Mamma."

"It's done shining on us for a while, Puddly. But somewhere else, it's shining on some other penguins, warming up their cold faces. And soon it will be our turn again. That's the circle of the sun. And until then, even though we can't see it or feel it, we can still know it. We can still remember it. We can still trust it will come back. Even in the coldest darkness, we can still really know that it is very much alive, this very moment, and shining brightly, somewhere else. And when we remember the sun, that helps us have a little bit of its warmth in our own hearts. A little bit of sunshine inside us, that we can just let shine, for ourselves and others, until the sun comes back to share its warmth with us again."

"Awwwe, I miss you, Mamma. Right now I can't feel the sun, but I can remember when I have felt it, and I can know that it will come back tomorrow. And I can let myself feel that inside. It's still shining, just as bright as ever. Just not on me. Maybe somewhere, far away, there's another penguin waddling all alone, that's smaller than me, and the sun is what helps that little penguin not give up. I don't want to keep them from having that warmth and that hope. I wouldn't want to keep the sun all to myself, even if I could. I do want to share it with the whole big world. I really do. Goodbye, sun. Right now, maybe there's a little penguin somewhere who is really happy to see you. I'm glad you're making them happy. And soon it will be my turn again. That's the circle of the sun."

And just then, for the briefest moment, underneath all of Puddly's miserableness and tiredness and coldness and sadness and scaredness, he felt just a little touch of happiness in his heart. It didn't last long, and it wasn't very strong. But it was enough. He felt a little more hope. A little more comfort. A little more okayness. And he felt a little less alone. That gave him the strength to start waddling onward again a little more, fighting the strong, harsh wind with every slow, heavy step.

"Just this next step, Puddly. You can do it. Just this next step."

And then, just for an instant, Puddly heard a sound in the wind. A sound he had never heard before. It sounded like, well, he didn't know what it sounded like, but he had heard a lot of kinds of wind and this wasn't wind. "Maybe it's the ocean! Maybe it's the sea!" He took a few more steps, and then heard it again, from somewhere in front of him. And then he started to smell smells he had never smelled before. He waddled forward cautiously, unable to see very far ahead at all because of the blowing snow. The sound grew louder, and he thought he saw less white and more of a moving gray in front of him. And then, right after a loud sound, he felt a spray of water on his face.

"I'm here! I'm here! This is the ocean! I made it to the water! I made it!" He brushed away the ice sprinkles from his face and took a few more cautious steps forward. Not far in front of him, he could see through the blowing snow a big gray, rolling, moving something. He didn't have words to describe it. Strange. New. Amazing. Powerful. Beautiful. Mysterious. But somehow, familiar. Natural. Normal. Home away from home. He was absolutely sure. This was the ocean.

"I made it! You did it, Puddly! You did it, feet!" He took a big breath and smelled the cold, fresh, moist, salty air. "I'm really here! I'm at the ocean!"

He stood there, mesmerized, looking through the blowing snow at the beautiful and powerful moving water. He suddenly shivered from the cold wind, and remembered he still had to find help. "I made it all the way to the ocean, but now what do I do? Where's Papa? Where's the fishing group? The sun has already set and it's already getting colder and darker and windier. And with all this blowing snow I can't see very far at all! Yuckle doodle! I really really have to find my papa, and fast! Papa! HELP! Papa! PAPA!"

Chapter 14
A Distant Sound

Usually on colder, windier days, as it started to get dark, Splashers swam farther out to sea where there wasn't any wind. But tonight, for some reason he felt like swimming up and down along the ice lands. As he swam, he could hear the water splashing around against the ice. Then, just for a moment, he thought he heard something else, off in the distance. He stopped and listened. Nothing.

"Probably just some ice moving," he thought. Then he swam down deep into the water, to practice holding his breath for the Big Swim.

Chapter 15
Hope

Puddly stood there, watching the dancing waves and trying to think things through. "It's so windy, there's no way Papa can hear me. And I don't know how far away he is, or if he's to my left or my right. Actually, I don't even know which is my left and which is my right, but even if I did, I still wouldn't know which way to go. What am I gonna do?"

With all the blowing snow and with it starting to get darker, even if he did go looking for the fishing group, he wouldn't be able to see far in front of him at all, and they wouldn't see him or hear him calling until he had almost reached them. The daylight was fading, the piercing wind was terribly cold and strong, and he knew he just didn't have much waddling left in him at all. He was all waddled out.

"I just really don't know what to do," he sniffled. "But I just can't, I just can't start waddling again when it's going to be dark soon, and there's just as much of a chance I'm getting farther away from Papa as there is I'm getting closer to him. I'm really sorry, but I just can't. I'm all done with waddling. I'm all done with trying to guess which way Papa went. I just don't have it in me to take one more step from this spot. I just really really don't."

Puddly started shouting with all his might, even though he knew his papa wasn't close enough to hear him. There was nothing else to do. "Papa! PAPA! Help! Are you there? Can anyone hear me? Please help me! HELP!"

~ ~ ~ ~ ~

When Splashers came up for air, he heard the sound again. It was just barely there, coming from the ice lands. It sounded like a penguin. He had seen penguins around now and then, and heard them calling to each other sometimes. This was a young one. And it was in trouble. Splashers swam over to investigate. "Hello? Hello? Where are you?" He swam back and forth along the edge of the ice, calling and listening. "Hello? Anyone there?"

~ ~ ~ ~ ~

Puddly was calling for his papa as loud as he could, but the wind was yelling even louder. "Papa will never hear me! I'm all alone and I'm scared and I'm cold, and I'm just gonna get colder and scareder. I just can't believe the mess I've gotten myself into! There's just no way I can find Papa before dark! There's just no way I can find any help tonight at all! I just can't see how I'm gonna be okay tonight. I just really, really can't."

Puddly couldn't quite tell if the little ice sickles on his cheeks were mostly from his tears or mostly from the sea spray. Once again he felt like just giving up, plopping down on the ice, and crying. There was no hope now. There was no chance of being saved. Why even try? But something in him just wouldn't let him. "Keep yelling, Puddly! Keep yelling as loud as you can! Don't give up! Even if you think it's totally hopeless, just don't give up! You can't give up!" So he kept calling, even though he couldn't really find any hope inside him at all.

"PAPA! Help! SOMEONE! Please help me! help! I need help! HELP!"

Suddenly, above the loud wind and sloshing water, Puddly heard a kind, reassuring voice, coming from somewhere in front of him.

"Hello? Can you hear me, little penguin?"

PART TWO
NEW FRIENDS

Chapter 16
A Dolphin Promise

"Can you hear me, little penguin? Are you okay?"

The voice sounded friendly, and after those first few moments of surprise, the truth was Puddly felt very, very relieved to know that, whoever was in front of him, he was no longer completely alone. "Who— who said that?" he asked. He thought he could barely see a shape down in the water that looked kind of like a huge fish, but with so much blowing snow it was hard to tell.

"I did. I heard you calling for help. Are you okay?"

"No, I'm really not okay at all," Puddly sniffled. "I'm lost and I'm scared and I'm cold and I'm tired and my feet just started waddling down Sunshine Hill and I can't find my papa and I shouldn't have left home and my mamma must be so worried by now and I'm gonna be in big big trouble if I ever make it home and if I don't make it home well that doesn't really sound so great either and I'm all alone and all I wanted was to go with him like Nightsong and Fuzzly got to when they were my age and it wasn't fair and I was so mad I stomped my foot and fell on my butt and I just wanted him to see that I AM big enough but now I'm lost and I'm scared and he has to be around here somewhere but the Night Winds are coming and it's getting dark fast and I'm getting cold and I'm really tired and I'm all alone in the whole world and— " He finally stopped to catch his breath. Then he started to cry. "I just really really don't know what to do."

"I'm really sorry, little penguin. Don't worry. I'm here and I'll help you."

"I'm, I'm NOT that little!"

"I didn't mean anything by it. Compared to us, all younger penguins are little. My name is Splashers. And I'm a dolphin."

"Hi, Splashers. You're a dull friend?"

Splashers laughed. "I hope not. But if you come a few steps closer, we can see and hear each other better."

"But, but I might fall in."

"You don't have to stand right at the edge of the ice if you don't want to. But you're a penguin and all penguins can swim."

"Well, I haven't ever swimmed yet."

"I'm sure when you try you'll see it's the easiest thing in the world for you. But I won't let you fall in."

Puddly was always told that penguins had to watch out for sea creatures, because some of them weren't very nice to penguins. But right now he didn't think he had a much better choice. He was in danger from the bitter cold Night Winds and couldn't just stand there alone until morning. And he felt the dull friend probably really was as kind as his voice, and really did want to help him. Puddly took a few cautious steps closer. He could see the dull friend better now, just a few steps in front of him down in the water. A big, blue-gray, strange looking sea creature.

"That's better," Splashers said. "You really are a young penguin, aren't you?"

"But I get a little older and bigger every single day! And a lot of nights too! What do you mean you're a dull friend?"

"Not a dull friend. I'm a dolphin."

"A dolphin? I thought I had heard about all the different kinds of fish. The good ones to eat and the giant ones that might try to eat me. But I've never heard of a dolphin before."

"Well, I'm definitely not a fish. Even the nicely decorated fish don't have much going on inside. Just 'food food food food food food food', as far as I can tell. I'm not a fish any more than you are fish. And I breathe air like you."

"Well why haven't I ever heard of dolphins before, Splashers?"

"I'm from a place far away, that's much more beautiful. I mean, more beautiful to me. Your world has its own kind of beauty, and I don't think penguins would like where I come from very much. But to me it's really beautiful there, and it's my home. There's probably never been another dolphin like me here before. That's probably why you've never heard of my kind. What's your name, young penguin?"

"Everyone calls me Puddly."

"Why do they call you that?"

"Mostly because it's my name, I guess. Hey, Splashers? Do you, do you eat penguins?"

"No, I don't eat penguins. Penguins and dolphins are sophisticated."

"We're what?"

"We're sophisticated. We're smarter and kinder and have bigger hearts than dumb fish. Sometimes I've watched penguins playing and swimming and catching fish and talking to each other. I've even tried to swim up and talk with some of them, but they always swim away scared and hop back on the ice before I can get close enough to have a friendly conversation."

"Yeah, we're always told to stay away from sea creatures. Some of them somehow get so confused they think we're food! Um, how do I know you're not one of those again?"

"Well, I'm glad you're being careful, Puddly. But I'm pretty good at jumping up out of the water, so if I had any interest in that, we wouldn't be talking right now."

Puddly took a step backwards.

"Don't worry, young penguin. I came to you because you were calling for help. I know what it's like to feel all alone and scared and unsure and lost. I really do. I'm here because I want to help you."

"Well, I could really use some help right about now, Splashers. Sure as snow. It's getting darker and the Night Winds are already getting bad and I can't find my papa and I'm just really all alone."

"Well, you're not alone any more, Puddly. And I'll do all I can to help you. You said your papa is somewhere not too far away?"

"I think so, Splashers. He brought a fishing group to the ocean, but I don't know where they are. By now they're probably done fishing, and are huddled together for the night somewhere."

"I've been swimming around this area for most of the day, Puddly. And I haven't seen them. I could swim up and down the edge of the ice calling to them, but it's getting darker and windier, and I've never seen penguins spend the night close to the water. So I don't think I would be able to see them and I don't think they could hear me. And it's too late for you to go looking for them. I think we just need to focus on helping you make it through the night."

"You mean you can't help me find my papa right now? I really don't want to be here alone all night, Splashers! I'm scared and I just really want to be with my papa!"

"I know you do, Puddly. I know it's not the same, but I'll be here with you."

"Thanks, Splashers," Puddly sniffled. "I'm really so glad you're here. You won't leave me all alone tonight?"

"No, Puddly. I won't leave you all alone."

"You promise?"

"Dolphin promise. And that's the strongest promise there is. Have you ever once heard of a dolphin breaking a promise?"

"No, I never once have," Puddly said, feeling comforted.

"Listen, Puddly. It's going to be a really cold and windy night, and it looks like you're already shivering a little. I don't think you can just stand there until morning."

"I don't really think so either, Splashers. But what else can we do?"

"I think we just have one real choice, Puddly. But I don't think you're going to like it very much."

Chapter 17
Just One Choice

"What choice, Splashers?" Puddly asked nervously. "What am I not gonna like very much?"

"Listen, Puddly. You penguins aren't made to just stand alone all night on the ice lands during the Night Winds. But you're specially made to be okay in icy cold water. I've seen penguins swim around for half a day just fine. It's not as windy down here in the water, and the ocean is so huge, it doesn't get colder at night the way the air does. I don't think we have another choice, Puddly. You'll have to spend the night in the water, where the Night Winds can't reach you nearly as much."

"In the wa-wa-water? But, but I've never EVER been in the water! I don't even know how to swim, Splashers! And it looks deep and dark and gray and pretty wet and it's all sploshing around all over the place and I don't know what kind of big mean giant fish monster might be in there waiting for me! I don't like that idea at all, Splashers. Nope. Not even a little. What else you got?"

"I know it feels scary, Puddly. But I can't think of another option, can you? You won't be as cold as you would be just standing alone out in the strong wind all night. And I'll be right here with you. No big fish will bother you with me around. It's the safest place for you to be tonight."

"That makes sense, Splashers, but I just really, really don't want to get in the water."

"I'm not going to pull you in, Puddly. This is something you have to do on your own."

Puddly thought about it. He was scared of standing there in the Night Winds all night, and he was scared of jumping into the ocean. But he knew which one he had to do. "Splashers, I know I have to get in the water. But I'm really not ready to just jump in yet. Maybe I could just start with moving a little closer to it."

"That sounds like a really good next thing to do, Puddly."

Puddly slowly inched forward until he was standing just one step away. The water was just a little jump down. The edge of the ice was about as tall as he was.

"So what do you think is the best thing to do now?" Splashers asked.

"Um, stall?"

"You can do it, Puddly. Just decide you're really going to do it, and jump in."

"But won't I just sink to the bottom, Splashers?"

"No, you're a penguin. Maybe your mind doesn't quite know how to swim yet, but your body already does. Penguin bodies are made for it. Just take a big breath and then jump in. I'll make sure you're safe, Puddly. You're made for swimming much more than you're made for waddling, and you waddled all the way here!"

"Yeah I really did, didn't I? Just barely! But what if I do sink down, Splashers? Will you be able to find me and lift me up?"

"We dolphins can see even better in the water than we can above it. Even if it's dark. We use sound seeing."

"What's sound seeing, Splashers?"

"We send out sounds and the way they come back to us lets us see everything in front of us. So I could find you easily, and then I could lift you up to the surface if you needed me to. But you won't sink, young penguin. You'll be amazed how natural and easy swimming will be for you."

"Well, will I have to swim all night? I'm really pretty tired already, Splashers."

"I've seen penguins in the water lots of times, Puddly. Sometimes they swim really fast and other times they just kind of float and relax. You don't have to work hard to float. It's natural for you and me. Look how I'm floating and talking to you, without having to work hard at all."

"So it's easy sneezy?"

"Easy sneezy."

"I just don't know for sure about this, Splashers."

"I understand that, Puddly. But we do know for sure it won't work for you to stay out alone in the bitter cold wind all night. And this is the only other option we can see. Would you rather wait until you're twice as cold and it's so dark you can't see me or the water at all?"

"I really don't want to do it later, Splashers. But I really don't want to do it now even more. My papa says the longer you put off doing something you dread, the harder it gets. Maybe I should just stand here and think about that for a while."

"You can do it, Puddly! Just jump in!"

Puddly knew he had no choice. No good choices anyway. He was getting tired of not having any good choices. He thought again about what his mamma sometimes said. "Courage isn't not being scared. It's doing what you know is good to do, even if it scares you. That's what being brave really is."

"Okay, Splashers. Let's just get it over with. I'm gonna do it!"

"You'll see, Puddly. It's a lot easier than you think."

Puddly started waddling around excitedly, getting up the courage to jump. "Okay, Splashers! Here I go!" He took in a big breath, closed his eyes, jumped up, and landed exactly where he had been standing. "Um, that was just kind of a little practice jump. This time I'll do it for real!"

He took another big breath, backed up, hopped forward twice, jumped up as high as he could, and landed exactly where he had been standing again. "Um, well, that was just another little practice jump, Splashers. I know I can do this! It's the scariest thing I've ever, ever done in my whole life, but I can do it! I know I can!"

Then Puddly took a little step forward, so that one foot was above the water. He took a deep breath, said "Here I Go! For real again!" and backed away from the edge. "I'm really sorry, Splashers. I'm just really really scared!"

"I really understand, Puddly. What if you sit down at the edge of the ice and then just kind of scoot in?"

"Okay, Splashers. That sounds a little better." Puddly sat down and scooted up to the very edge of the ice and closed his eyes. "Here

I go! One, two, threeeeeeeee!" He opened his eyes, and was still sitting there. "Yuckle doodle! Puddly Sunfacer Furfoot! It's okay to be scared, but you know this is what you need to do, so just do it!" He took a few deep breaths and then took the biggest breath he had ever taken. "Okay, Splashers. This really is it, sure as snow! Be ready to save me! One, two, THREEEEEEEEEEEE!"

With a little splash, Puddly plopped into the icy water, sank down just a little, and then his head popped up above the surface right in front of Splashers. He started penguin paddling frantically, and realized he wasn't sinking at all. He was swimming.

Chapter 18
Straight Talk

"I'm doing it! I'm swimming!" Puddly said as he frantically splashed around in front of Splashers. "Look at me! I'm swimming! I can swim! I really can!"

"See, Puddly?" Splashers said. "It's natural for a penguin. Now see if you can relax a little. Stop trying so hard, and just let yourself float."

Puddly stopped splashing around so frantically, and started moving more gently and calmly. "Hey, this is easy sneezy!"

"How does the water feel, Puddly?"

"Well, it's pretty wet! But you're right, Splashers. So far it feels a lot less cold and windy than being up there on the ice. It almost feels warm compared to that."

"Good. It might start to feel a little colder after a while, but the wind isn't as strong down here, and with your thick penguin padding keeping you warmer in water, it won't be nearly as cold for you as up on the ice. And I bet if you try you could move even less, and still keep floating."

Puddly tried moving a little less. "Hey, I'm doing it, Splashers! I don't have to move much at all! This isn't even tiring! Swimming is way easier than waddling! And it still feels warmer!"

"You're doing great, Puddly."

"I just can't believe I'm swimming in the ocean! With a dolphin! I guess when a day starts, you can never really know for sure just where it's going to end up. So what's our plan now, Splashers? We just stay here in the water all night and then in the morning we try to find my papa?"

"I think that's all we can do, Puddly. Could you tell me what happened again? Maybe a little slower this time?"

"Sure, Splashers. Well, I got really mad at my papa. He wouldn't let me go with the fishing group because he said I wasn't big enough yet. Even though Nightsong and Fuzzly got to go when they were my age. They always talk about how amazing it was, and Papa wouldn't even let me go! It wasn't fair, and I kept asking and arguing with him, and then he got frustrated with me. Sometimes he tells me not to give up, and then when I don't give up and I keep asking him after he says no, he gets mad that I didn't give up! So he got all mad and he just wouldn't give me a chance, and then I stormed off to the top of Sunshine Hill. That's my very own hill. And I think my feet were even madder than me because before I knew it, they just started waddling down Sunshine Hill towards Sea Way Hill and the ocean. And when your feet are waddling away from you, if you don't follow them you'll just fall on your butt!"

"So your feet just started waddling, Puddly?"

"Well that's how it felt. I just suddenly noticed that's what they were doing."

"They just decided by themselves?"

"Well, I don't remember telling them to do it, Splashers."

"So who do you think did?"

"I don't know, but if I ever find out I'm gonna give them a talking to! They got me in a big mess!"

"Puddly, who told your feet to start waddling? Really."

"Well, I guess I did, Splashers. I was just so mad. Then at Sea Way Hill I decided the best thing to do was catch up with the fishing group and tell my papa everything. But I was too slow and they were too fast and I was too tired and they were too far ahead and the wind was too strong and they just couldn't hear me at all. And soon I couldn't even see them anymore because of all the blowing snow, so I just tried my best to get to the ocean. I just barely barely made it, and then you came and helped me. I made such a mess of things, Splashers. I was just really mad and didn't think things through too good."

"Puddly, it sounds like your papa was just trying to keep you safe."

"I know, Splashers. It's just that I'm really really tired of being small for my age. It's not fair!"

"I know that's hard for you sometimes, Puddly. But by having such a big fit and not thinking things through, you got yourself into a situation that wasn't safe."

"I know, Splashers. I was really stupid."

"Not stupid. You were smart enough to know it wasn't a good idea. You were just stubbornly demanding to have your own way, even if it meant putting yourself in danger and making other penguins worry about you. Puddly, you can't control how big you are on the outside. But you CAN control how big you are on the inside. What you did, having a fit and waddling off towards the ocean by yourself— that wasn't very big. You were saying you were big enough to go, and then you chose to do something really, really small."

"Ouch, Splashers. That doesn't feel good to hear at all. Whose side are you on anyway?"

"Being on your side means always agreeing with everything you say?"

"Right, so if you could just stick with that from now on, that would be great."

"Puddly, a friend doesn't help you not see. A friend helps you see. A friend is straight with you when it seems good to be. But someone who always agrees with you just so you don't have to hear something you don't want to hear, that's not a real friend. Because that doesn't really help you."

"I guess that's true, Splashers."

"If you really want to be big, then be big in the only way you can control. On the inside. Even if you don't like what I'm saying, do you know what I mean?"

"Yeah, I know what you mean, Splashers. I know my papa was just doing the best he could to keep me safe and to bring back all the fish he could for the valley. And I wasn't very nice to him, Splashers. Before I stormed off to my hill I told him he was mean and I didn't like him. I hope he knows, I hope I get a chance to tell him, I didn't really mean it. And I'm really sorry."

"You will, Puddly."

"You really think so, Splashers?"

"I really think so, Puddly. I'm sure he already knows you didn't mean it, but you'll get a chance to tell him yourself soon."

"I hope I do, Splashers. I just really hope I do."

Chapter 19
Ripples in the Water

Puddly paddled with one flipper, making little ripples as he spun around in a circle until he faced Splashers again. "Swimming is kind of fun, Splashers! I was so scared to jump in the water, but once I did, it wasn't nearly as scary as waiting to do it was." He paddled with his other flipper and spun around in a circle the other way. "I'm really glad I got in the water when I did, though. Is it just gonna get darker and darker tonight, Splashers?"

"Don't worry, Puddly. The moon will come up before long, and it's going to be big and bright tonight."

"That's really good to hear, Splashers. I wasn't too excited about floating here all night in this big huge ocean without being able to see at all. Hey, Splashers? You haven't told me yet why you came here. You said you're from a place far away that's really warm and beautiful. So what are you doing so far from your home? Did you get mad at your papa and run off too?"

"No, nothing like that, Puddly. Dolphins don't really have papas. But I didn't want to leave my mamma and my brother, Poptail. I didn't want to leave my home."

"Then what happened, Splashers? Why did you leave?"

"Well, I was just swimming around the reef, like I often did, when—"

"What's a reef?"

"A coral reef. It's a beautiful, beautiful place that has all kinds of amazing fish and plants and sea animals of every color and shape you could imagine. Reefs are some of the most amazing places there are. I love to swim through them because they're so peaceful and beautiful, and because every time I do, I see something amazing I've never seen before. To me, reefs are the most beautiful, special places in the whole world."

"Wow. Reefs sound really amazing, Splashers."

"They really are, Puddly. My mamma says there used to be a lot more of them, but there aren't as many now. And it's just a really special thing to swim around one. So I was just swimming along, exploring the reef, and the next thing I knew I was caught in a fishing net."

"You were? Wow! That's unbelievable, Splashers! What's a fishing net?"

"Well, where I live, you see them sometimes, and we all know to stay away from them. But this one caught me by surprise. Land people use them to catch fish and other sea creatures. Fishing nets trap you and you can't get free."

"What are land people?"

They live on the land, and they walk on two feet like you do, but they aren't nearly as good at swimming as you and me. And sometimes they catch fish in the ocean, but they can't catch fish as well as dolphins or penguins can, so if they want to catch a lot of fish they have to use big nets."

"Wow. I never knew about land people, Splashers. And what's a net again?"

"It's something that traps you so you can't get free."

"How does it do that?"

"Well, imagine a whole lot of really tall, thin ice sickles, really close to each other, all around you. Then imagine a lot of sideways ice sickles too, going across the tall ones. You wouldn't be able to get out. A net is kind of like that, except each of those ice sickles can bend and tighten around you so you can hardly move."

"Wow, that sounds really scary, Splashers!"

"It really was, Puddly. Suddenly there was a net around me, and I couldn't get out and I couldn't even come up for air. And then, just when I didn't think I could hold my breath any more, the net came up above the water and I could breathe again. But then the land people pulled the net up into their boat."

"Really? They did? I just can't even believe that, Splashers! What's a boat?"

"Well, a boat is kind of like an iceberg that land people make, and they use them to float on the water and move through it really fast."

"Wow, Splashers. The world sure is a lot bigger than I ever knew it was. So they put you on their boat?"

"And then they kept me in a really small space, hardly bigger than me. And then the boat started moving really fast, farther and farther from my home. And every day it got a little colder. And sometimes it would rain, but then it got so cold that instead of rain there was just snow."

"What's rain, Splashers?"

"That's what snow is when it's warmer. Little drops of water falling down everywhere."

"Kind of like a giant sky sneeze?"

"Kind of like that, Puddly. And then there started to be ice in the water. More every day. Then one day a big storm came and the waves got really big and the boat tipped over on its side. That's how I got free."

"Double wow, Splashers! I thought I had a big adventure today, but you had the biggest one I've ever heard of! What were the land people gonna do with you?"

"I don't know, Puddly. I don't think they wanted to hurt me, but they put me in too small a space, and they took me away from my family, without even asking if I wanted to go."

"That wasn't a very nice thing to do, Splashers. Are land people bad?"

"I think most of them are good, Puddly. A lot of them are really friendly and kind to dolphins. But some of them seem like they don't really care much about how what they do affects the rest of us. Or maybe they just don't realize it. Either way, it's kind of hard for us dolphins to understand, because we believe everything we do sends out ripples in the water. So we try to send out ripples of fun and laughter and playfulness and kindness and helping and heart, because that feels better in our own hearts, and those are just the kinds of ripples we like to bump into ourselves."

"It doesn't sound like the land people who took you sent out very nice ripples, Splashers. So how long ago did you escape? How long have you been here?"

"Well, it was almost Big Moon when I escaped, and it was Big Moon last night. And there's been one Big Moon in between."

"Really? That's a long time to be somewhere you don't want to be, Splashers. Why haven't you gone back yet?"

"Well, it's a really long swim, and I've just been waiting for the right time."

"And what makes it the right time, Splashers?"

"That's kind of complicated, Puddly. There are a lot of important dolphin things to consider, that a penguin probably wouldn't understand."

"Like what?"

"You sure do ask a lot of questions, don't you, Puddly?"

"Why do you say that, Splashers? Do I really? Mostly just when I want to know something. Like what complicated things?"

"Well, there's things like the changing ocean currents that can make it twice as fast or twice as slow to get where you want to go. That kind of thing. So I'm just waiting for the best time."

"Wow, you sure do know a lot about the ocean, Splashers. I would have thought if you really want to swim somewhere, you just start swimming, with all your heart, and don't really stop until you get there. But it sounds like it's a whole lot more complicated than that. So when do you think the best time will be?"

"I really don't know, Puddly," Splashers said quietly. "But every day, it's feeling farther and farther away."

Chapter 20
Sky Stories

"How are you doing, Puddly?" Splashers asked. "It looks like you're shivering a little."

"Well, I'm a little cold, Splashers. But if I was just standing up there on the ice in that awful wind all night, it would be a lot worse. I'm just really glad you found me." Puddly looked up at the sky. "Hey, Splashers, look! Now that it's getting dark the stars are waking up! I love the stars."

"Me too, Puddly."

"Sometimes, back home in Penguin Valley, when it's late at night and everyone is sleeping, and the only sounds are the wind and my papa snoring, well sometimes I wake up and I just watch the stars slowly moving across the sky. It doesn't really look like they're moving. But if you look at where they are, and then close your eyes for a while, then if you wait long enough, when you open them again all the stars have moved a little. You can't ever catch them doing it, but they are, sure as snow. They must be really patient to move so slow like that."

"They must be, Puddly. Sometimes I like to float on my back and just watch the stars. And once in a while, I'll even see a teardrop star and make a wish."

"What's a teardrop star, Splashers?"

"Well, it comes from an old story we dolphins have about the sky. Do you want to hear it?"

"Sure, Splashers! I don't know any dolphin stories at all!"

"Okay, Puddly. Here it is. A long time ago, at the beginning of the world, before there was any land, or any stars or moon or sun, or any other animals, there were two great dolphins. The first father dolphin and the first mother dolphin. And they could live forever. And every year they got bigger and bigger. And so did their hearts. Every year they loved each other more and they loved the ocean more and they loved the dark quiet sky more and they loved the whole beautiful new world more. But after many, many years of getting bigger every year, they finally became so big that even the entire ocean was too small for them."

"Wow, Splashers. They must have been two really big dolphins!"

"And finally, they got so big they just couldn't stay here anymore. So they decided to swim into the sky. And their big hearts made them shine really brightly. The father dolphin became the sun and the mother dolphin became the moon. And they've been up there for longer than anyone can know, and they'll stay up there forever, shining their light down into the world."

"That makes my heart smile, Splashers."

"Mine too, Puddly. And the father sun dolphin, he shines just during the day, and warms up the whole world. And the mother moon dolphin, she shines mostly at night so that she can help us find our way in the darkness, when we need it the most. They do that for the world because they love it and want to help it. But ever since they swam into the sky, the only time they can see each other is when they're both up in the sky at the same time. And sometimes their big hearts are overflowing with sadness because they can't be together. And other times, their big hearts are overflowing with happiness because they get to share their light with this beautiful, amazing, precious world. And sometimes their sadness and happiness are so strong, they cry. Long ago, their sparkling tears spread throughout the whole sky and became the stars. And then, when the sky was so full of stars that there wasn't room for any more, their tears started to come down into the world, and give us rain. And once in a while, you can see one of their star tears fall down from the sky. And that's what dolphins call a teardrop star."

"Wow, that's a really great story, Splashers! We don't have any stories like that at all. But once Nightsong told Fuzzly some jokes, and he laughed so hard he turned the snow yellow. Not really the same kind of thing though, overall. But Mamma does say that there's a little bit of sunshine glowing in every penguin's heart. And that can keep us warm when the sun seems gone. And it can remind us that the sun is always shining bright, never too far away, even when it hasn't shined on us for a while."

"I like that, Puddly."

"Me too, Splashers. Thinking of that helped me keep waddling to the ocean when I really wanted to just plop my butt down in the snow. But right now it's not really keeping me very warm."

"I'm sorry you're cold, Puddly. You're still shivering some."

"I'm okay, Splashers. I'm just really really glad you're here with me. Hey Splashers?"

"Yeah, Puddly?"

"Are you double sure you won't leave me alone tonight?"

"I'm double sure, Puddly. I'll stay right here with you the whole night. I gave you a dolphin promise, remember?"

"I remember. I think I just kind of wanted to hear you say it again. Some things are just nice to hear twice. Hey Splashers, want to hear the jokes Nightsong told Fuzzly?"

"Sure, Puddly."

"Okay! I don't really know if a dolphin will think they're funny, but here they are. Hey Splashers. How many snowflakes does it take to make a snow mountain?"

"I don't know, Puddly. How many?"

"Just one. But it would be kind of a small mountain. Hey Splashers. How many penguins does it take standing on each other's shoulders to reach all the way to the moon?"

"I don't know. How many?"

"Just two. But they would have to be kind of tall penguins. Hey Splashers. How many penguins would it take to eat all the fish in the ocean?"

"Just one? But it would have to be kind of a big penguin."

"I guess you heard that one already. How about this one? Hey Splashers. If you have the biggest sea monster in the whole world, and the meanest sea monster in the world, and you put them together, what do you get?"

"I don't know, Puddly. What do you get?"

"Away fast! Hey Splashers."

"Are there a lot more of these, Puddly?"

"Yup! Nightsong told Fuzzly a bunch of them! Hey Splashers. How much water is in the whole world?"

"I don't know, Puddly. How much water is in the whole world?"

"All of it! Hey Splashers. What do you call a shell if it's a girl?"

"What do you call a shell if it's a girl?"

"Yeah. What do you call a shell if it's a girl?"

"I don't know, Puddly. What do you call a shell if it's a girl?"

"Shelly! Hey Splashers. What do you call a shell if it's a girl and it's not really moving much?"

"I don't know, Puddly. What?"

"Still Shelly! Hey Splashers. If I have two shells, and someone takes one, how many would I have?"

"One?"

"Nope! I'd have two! Because if someone takes one of my shells, I'm gonna take it right back!

Okay. I think that's all of them I can remember for now."

"Those were pretty good, Puddly."

"Well I think maybe they're funnier when my sister tells them to my brother. If you were Fuzzly you'd be laughing yellow by now. Splashers, can I ask you something for real?"

"Sure, Puddly."

"Don't make fun of me for asking, okay?"

"I won't, Puddly. What do you want to ask?"

"Splashers, what's a shell?"

"You don't know what a shell is, Puddly?"

"I don't think so. I was a little too shy to ask Nightsong or Fuzzly."

"Well, some sea creatures have a strong, hard protection around them, kind of like a thin rock or a thin chunk of ice, that wraps around their body and makes it harder for them to be eaten. Most of them live their whole lives in their shells, and it keeps them safer."

"Wow. That sounds like a really nice thing to have, Splashers. I wish I had a shell. Then when someone says I'm too little, or pokes me with other words I don't like, it wouldn't hurt my feelings so much. Awwwe, but then I wouldn't get to feel the sunshine as much either."

"That's true, Puddly. And sea creatures with shells are mostly a lot heavier and slower and clumsier. They can't move around very well. It's harder for them to get to where they want to go, because they have to carry around that heavy shell with them everywhere."

"That wouldn't be too much fun, Splashers. So the more of a shell you carry around with you, the heavier and harder and slower it is to get where you want to be. And the less you can feel anything when you finally get there, or even on the way. That wouldn't feel very good to live like that day after day, Splashers. Sometimes my feelings really get hurt, but I get to feel a lot of good things too. So I guess really I'm pretty lucky I don't have a shell."

"I think you're right, Puddly. I think you're right."

Chapter 21
Moon Rise

"Look, Puddly. The moon is coming up."

"Wow, it's beautiful, Splashers! I've never seen the moon rise up out of the ocean before. It looks really really big!"

"I've been looking at the moon a lot lately," Splashers said quietly. "Sometimes I like to think of my mamma and Poptail looking at it too. And that helps me feel connected to them."

"What do you mean, Splashers?"

"Well, maybe sometimes when they're looking at the moon, they're thinking about me. And maybe they send their heart ripples all the way up to the moon and right back down to me. And I can send my heart ripples back to them. Even though they feel so far away, we're under the same moon. And that helps me feel more like we're connected. And maybe there are times when we're even looking at the moon and thinking about each other at the same time. When I think about that, it helps me get through these long, cold nights."

"That's a really nice way to see things, Splashers. Maybe right now my mamma is watching the moon rise. And maybe she's thinking about me and wondering where I am and sending me heart ripples. Awwwe, I'm really sorry, Mamma. I'm here, and I'm okay. Splashers is keeping me really really safe. And tomorrow, we'll find Papa and he'll get me back home to you. I know you must be so worried about me, Mamma. I'm a little cold and I'm pretty tired, but I'm really okay. And I'll be home just as soon as I can. Just like Splashers will be. We promise, Mamma. Right, Splashers? We promise."

Splashers didn't say anything.

"Right, Splashers? We'll both be home just as soon as we can, sure as snow. We promise, don't we, Splashers? Just as soon as we can."

Splashers was still silent, looking down at the water.

"What is it, Splashers? What's wrong?"

"Puddly, I need to tell you something."

"Sure, Splashers. You can tell me anything. What is it?"

"Well, to tell you the truth, and to really fully admit it to myself, I'm… scared."

"You? You're scared? What are you scared of, Splashers?"

"I'm scared to start the Big Swim home, Puddly. That's the real reason I haven't left yet. It's going to take me a really long time, swimming through strange new waters. I really don't like being here in this cold, lonely world, so far from home. But at least I know what to expect here. At least I feel safe. Even though I'm alone and its cold and it doesn't feel like home, it's familiar now. I know what's here. And the Big Swim is going to be a lot of not knowing. I don't know how long it will take, or what the different waters will be like, or what I will find. So I haven't been able to get myself to start it yet. I just keep finding excuses to wait. But I wasn't being honest with you earlier, when I said there were good reasons. There really aren't. I'm sorry about that, Puddly. I just felt too ashamed to admit the truth. The truth is, I'm scared."

"Awwwe, it's okay, Splashers. I would be scared too. I'm sure anyone would be. You know what my mamma says? She says having a courageous heart doesn't mean you don't feel pretty scared sometimes. It means you still do what you know in your heart is the best thing to do, even if it really really scares you. She says that's what being brave is really about."

"Could you say that again, Puddly?"

"Sure, Splashers. She says being brave doesn't mean not being scared. It means even if it scares you more than anything, you still do what you know in your heart is good to do. That's what true courage really is."

"I never really thought of it that way, Puddly. I've been trying really hard not to be scared, and I've been waiting to start the Big Swim until I'm not. But the truth is, I don't know if that day will ever come. So to just accept that I'm scared, instead of fighting with that or waiting until I'm not, to just really let myself be scared and still do what I know is good to do anyway— I really like that."

"Yeah, Splashers. So you just know that maybe you'll feel scared and alone sometimes on your long swim, but you still do it anyway. Because you really know in your heart that it's good to go home to your family. Being scared doesn't mean you aren't brave. Being scared is what gives you the chance to be really brave. That's what my mamma says."

"That feels kind of like a relief, Puddly. Just forgetting about trying not to be scared. I haven't had any luck with that anyway. So just starting with 'Of course I'm scared.' And then just deciding to really do what I need to do anyway, even though it will scare me."

"Just like when I jumped in the water, Splashers. I was really, really scared, and I didn't know what would happen. It took me a lot of tries, but I finally did it." Puddly paddled backwards a little, and then forwards again. "And it turns out, swimming is easy sneezy!"

"You know, Puddly, there's something about what you're saying that really feels right to me. It's true I can't really know what's waiting for me on the Big Swim. I can't control the sky or the waves or the currents or what I might find on my way home. I can't wait around here until I know what's going to happen, because I can't ever know before it happens. I just have to go for it. I just have to swim into the unknown to get home. The only way for me to get where I want to be is to go through where I don't want to be. To go through where I've never been before. And it doesn't really matter that I'm scared. I still know it's good to do it. And that's really all I need to know. You've really given me something to think about, Puddly."

"I'm glad, Splashers. I want you to get back home where you belong. And I know you can do it." Puddly looked up at the endless night sky and shivered. "I want to get home too, Splashers. I really, really do."

"I know you do, Puddly," Splashers said softly. "You will soon. How are you doing?"

"I'm still pretty okay I guess. But I'm just really ready for the sun to warm my face again. Right now that feels like a long long ways away. But I know it will be our turn to feel the sunshine again before too long. Mamma says that's the circle of the sun. Hey Splashers, do you want to hear a little poem my mamma sometimes says at sleep time when it's really cold?"

"Sure, Puddly."

"It's dark and it's cold
But it won't be for long
The colder the night
The sweeter the dawn

Soon all your shivers
They will be gone
The colder the night
The sweeter the dawn

Rest all your worries
For you can count on
The colder the night
The sweeter the dawn

Now close your eyes
And let your heart sing its song
The colder the night
The sweeter the dawn

It's time for warm dreams
Drift away with a yawn
The colder the night
The sweeter the dawn"

Puddly yawned a big, slow yawn and his eyes started to close. He caught himself, opened them, and paddled a little to make sure he was still floating. "Did you like my mamma's poem, Splashers?"

"It was a really nice poem, Puddly."

"I think so too, Splashers." Puddly yawned again. "I love my mamma's poems."

"I have an idea, Puddly," Splashers said, moving beside him. "Do you want to see if you can scoot onto my flipper and lean back against me for a while? Then you could just really relax, and maybe watch the stars moving."

"Really, Splashers? You wouldn't mind?"

"No, I wouldn't mind, Puddly. Let's give it a try and see how it works for you."

"Okay, Splashers. We can try it."

Puddly scooted onto Splashers' flipper and leaned back against his side. Splashers tilted a little so Puddly could rest with his head just above the water. "How's that, Puddly?"

"Really good, Splashers. Thanks! Leaning back like this I can almost see the whole sky!"

"Do you want to close your eyes for a while, Puddly, and then you can open them later to see if the stars have moved?"

"That sounds like a good idea," Puddly said, closing his eyes. Then he opened them again. "Thank you, Splashers. For everything. If you hadn't found me and helped me, well I don't really want to think about that too much."

"You're welcome, Puddly. Close your eyes now, so you can open them later and see if the stars have moved."

"Okay, Splashers. Just for a little bit, to give them a chance to sneak forward a little."

Puddly closed his eyes, and in no time at all, he was fast asleep. Splashers stayed as still as he could until morning, watching the moon and stars slowly move across the night sky, and thinking about finally starting the Big Swim back home, even though it scared him.

PART THREE
THE PULL OF HOME

Chapter 22
Sun Rise

Puddly awoke feeling the warm morning sun on his face. He took in a big breath of the fresh, crisp ocean air, stretched, and then scooted off Splashers' flipper into the water.

"Good morning, young penguin," Splashers said, as he turned to face Puddly.

"Good morning, Splashers. I guess maybe I kind of fell asleep a little. Did you just stay still all night? Just for me?"

"I didn't mind, Puddly. You really needed to sleep. You did a lot of waddling yesterday, and you'll have a lot to do today too. Now let's get you out of the water. Can you hop onto the ice?"

"I don't think so, Splashers. The ice is as tall as I am, and I can't jump that high yet. I will one day. I'll jump as high as any penguin. But not just yet."

"Then let me help you a little." Splashers put his tail under Puddly and slowly lifted him up onto the ice.

"Thanks, Splashers! That was fun! It feels a little funny standing on solid ice again after being in the water all night." Then he turned towards the sun and closed his eyes for a few moments. "Mamma's poem was right, Splashers. The colder the night, the sweeter the dawn. It's so good to feel the sunshine on my face again. When the sun disappeared yesterday, behind that selfish cloud, I wasn't so sure I ever would. Thank you, Splashers! You really saved my life!"

"You're welcome, Puddly. Now let's see if we can find your papa and the fishing group. Can you see them anywhere?"

Puddly looked around. He could see a lot better now than when he had reached the ocean the evening before, but he still didn't see any signs of the fishing group. "I can't see them anywhere, Splashers. And I can see pretty far now that the blowing snow is gone. I wonder where they are."

Splashers jumped up high out of the water a few times to see if he could spot them.

"Wow, you sure can jump high, Splashers! Do you see them? Do You?"

"No, I don't see them either, Puddly. Last night was so windy and cold, maybe they spent the night farther away. Or maybe they even decided to go back home. Does that sound like something they might do?"

"Maybe, Splashers. If they did, they probably would have spent the night at Sea Way Hill, where they could get out of the wind. But maybe they're still near the ocean somewhere, not that far away."

"Puddly, how about if you stay here and I'll swim up a ways and look for them? And if I don't see them I'll come back and check on you and then look for them the other way."

"Well, that seems like a pretty good idea, Splashers. But I just really don't want you to leave me here all alone."

"I know, Puddly. But we need to try to find them. I won't be gone long."

"Well, could I maybe go with you?"

"I'm sorry, Puddly. But if they are still at the ocean, I need to swim as fast as I can to try to catch them before they leave. I'll be right back, okay?"

"Okay, Splashers. If you have to."

Splashers took off faster than Puddly had ever imagined. He waited anxiously, and kept looking off into the distance, hoping to see the fishing group. "Where are you, Papa? I really need to find you."

Before long, Splashers was back. "No sign of them that way, Puddly. Are you doing okay?"

"Yeah, I'm okay, Splashers. You can swim really fast! Well maybe you'll see them the other way. I really hope so."

"Me too, Puddly. I'll be right back."

Puddly watched Splashers speed off again. "Awwwe, hurry back, Splashers. It's nice to be alone sometimes, just me and the sunshine. But this morning, I'd really much rather stay close to you."

Soon he saw Splashers swimming up to him again. "Did you see them, Splashers? Did you see my papa?"

Splashers shook his head. "I'm sorry, Puddly. They just aren't here. Maybe they were, but they aren't now. I jumped up into the air a lot to get a better view, and still couldn't see them anywhere."

"Awwwe, that's really too bad, Splashers. I was really really hoping you'd see them."

"I know, Puddly. Me too."

"Splashers, it doesn't really make sense that they would spend the night near the ocean and then leave so early, before they could catch more fish. Maybe they really did leave last night. Even with them huddled together, it would have been terribly cold so close to the ocean. I think they must have decided to leave early and go back to Sea Way Hill out of the wind."

"It's looking that way, Puddly. And now that the wind is calmer, I think if they had been somewhere along the water this morning I would have seen their tracks in the snow."

"Then what are we gonna do, Splashers? What the blizzard are we gonna do?"

"Well, let's think this through, Puddly. Do you think they'll come looking for you when they find out you're gone?"

"Sure as snow, Splashers! My papa won't ever stop looking for me until he finds me! Not ever! If they did spend the night at Sea Way Hill then they'll get back to Penguin Valley before high sun today. Then they'll find out I'm gone, and my papa will start looking for me right away! Probably other penguins are already looking for me, but it was too cold last night for them to go very far. But I don't know if anyone will think that I might have gotten all the way to the ocean. And even if they do, it's a big area where I could be and it takes penguins a lot longer to waddle than it takes you to swim. So I don't really know how soon they'll find me, Splashers. I just know my papa won't ever give up until he does. Not ever."

"I believe you, Puddly. I know he'll do everything he can to find you. And it sounds like other penguins will be looking too. But I don't think we can count on anyone finding you here today. And maybe not tomorrow either."

"Yuckle doodle! That's not so good, Splashers! I really want to be with my papa again! And my mamma. And Night Song. And even Fuzzly! I just want to go home!" Puddly started to cry. "I just really, really want to go home!"

"I know you do, Puddly," Splashers said gently. "It's really okay to feel sad. We dolphins say it's all of our happy and sad tears that make the ocean salty. But we also know there's a time for tears and a time for focus, and this is a time for focus, Puddly. So that we can make the best decisions we possibly can, as soon as we can."

"I understand, Splashers," Puddly sniffled. "I'll try to focus. What do you think we should do?"

"Puddly, you were shivering some last night in the water. It was warmer for you than standing out in the Night Winds, but you aren't really made to be in the icy cold water all night long, night after night. So I really don't think it's a good idea for you to do that two or three nights in a row. And it will definitely be too cold and windy for you to be out of the water all night."

"But if I can't be IN the water, and I can't be OUT of the water, what's left, Splashers? Do you think I should start waddling back home?"

"Well, the wind is a lot calmer now, but it looks like a lot of snow has blown in. If it's like that most of the way to Penguin Valley, it's going to really slow you down and make things a lot harder for you. It might be too much for you to make it all the way back home before dark."

"But Splashers, what else is there? Either I start going back, but it might be too much for me to waddle through all the new snow and I might not make it before dark, or I stay here with you another night or two and maybe get too cold! We don't know how soon they'll come looking for me all the way here at the ocean, and even when they do, we don't know how long before they find me! Double yuckle doodle! I don't feel good about my choices at all! I messed up so bad! What do I do, Splashers? What do I do?"

Splashers looked like he was thinking about something very serious.

"What is it, Splashers?"

"I just need to do some thinking, Puddly. I'm going to swim around a little, but I'll mostly be where you can see me. I won't be long."

"Really, Splashers? Do you have to? Well, please don't go too far."

"I won't, Puddly. Dolphin promise."

Chapter 23
A Courageous Heart

Puddly stood at the edge of the ice and watched Splashers swimming around, not too far away. A few times, Splashers dove underwater for a while, and Puddly got a little nervous until he could see him again. "I don't much like being left alone again in the middle of nowhere," he said quietly. "Please hurry up, Splashers." Before long, he saw Splashers swimming back to him.

"Puddly, I've been thinking about something," Splashers said, looking up at Puddly as he reached the edge of the ice. "I've asked myself every day, why did this happen to me. Why did I get taken so far away from my family and friends, so far from my home. I don't know if there's an answer. Maybe I was just in the wrong place at the wrong time. Maybe things just happen sometimes. But I do know that if I hadn't been here, you probably wouldn't have made it through the night. I don't know if that's why I ended up here. I have no idea. But this morning, this morning I've decided to believe it. I've decided to believe that I got dragged all the way here, to this strange and cold and lonely place so far from my home, to save your life, Puddly. That's what I've decided to believe. And it looks like I'm not finished doing that yet."

"Wow, Splashers. That's an awful lot of trouble to go through to save my life. But what more can you do?"

Splashers was silent for a moment. "I don't know how far I can get. Maybe not far at all. But I can try."

"Try what, Splashers?"

"Listen, Puddly. I really don't think you should try to stay here another night or two, or more. In the water or out of it. I just don't know if your body could stay strong enough to make it all the way back home. And we aren't sure how soon your papa will find you here. It might not be soon enough. So I think you have to start heading home now. Do you agree with me?"

"I don't much like it, Splashers. But I think you're probably right."

"So that leaves us with two choices, Puddly. You can struggle through all the new snow by yourself, which will make you a lot more tired a lot sooner, or I can try to scoot along in front of you, the best I can, for as long as I can."

Puddly was confused. "But Splashers, you're a dolphin! You're made for the sea! You said that I'm not made to be in the cold water all the time, and I know you aren't made to be out of the water even a little! What you're saying doesn't make any sense."

"You're right that it won't be easy or natural for me, Puddly. But maybe I can do it just for a little while. Just long enough. If I can lead the way some, and flatten down the snow for you, that will help you get farther more easily, so that you'll have more strength and time to get all the way home before dark. We just don't have a better choice, Puddly. I know in my heart, I have to try."

"I just don't even know what to say, Splashers. I just can't believe you would even think about doing something like that for me. You already saved my life last night. Now you want to try to scoot along in front of me to help make sure I make it home? But won't you be really cold? And get really, really tired?"

"It's okay for me to be cold and tired, if it helps you make it home."

"You really think you can scoot through the snow a little ways, Splashers? That seems like it would be so hard for you."

"I'm sure I can do it for as long as I can do it, Puddly. And when I can't go any more, then you'll have to make it on your own. But maybe I can flatten down the snow for a ways, so you'll have more strength left to make it home before the Night Winds come."

"You mean when you can't go any more because you need to turn around to make it back here to the ocean?"

Splashers looked away. "Yes, so I can turn around and make it back to the water," he said softly.

"So you'll be okay?"

Splashers looked away again. "I'll be okay, Puddly. What's more important is, you'll be home and safe."

"But Splashers, why is that more important than you staying safe in the water, to make sure you get back to your mamma and brother?"

"I can't explain it, Puddly. I just know in my heart it is. And a dolphin's heart is one of the best places there is to know something. It's settled. I'm not changing my mind. I'm going with you, as far as I can."

"Well, okay, Splashers. But I really don't feel too good about you leaving the water."

"I know, Puddly. But I really do feel good about knowing I will have helped you get back home safe with your family. It just wouldn't feel right in me not to try. I'll be right back, and then we'll get going."

"You're gonna leave me again? I'll be waiting right here, okay, Splashers? Please don't be gone too long."

"I won't, Puddly."

Splashers swam out to the other side of a nearby iceberg. He looked up at the morning moon, still in the sky.

"Mamma. Poptail. All my friends. Right now, we're really far away from each other. But we're under the same moon. Maybe we're even looking at it at the same time. I need to feel your strength. I need to feel your heart ripples. I'm okay, Mamma. But I need to know you're with me. I've been here so long because I was too scared to start the Big Swim home. But now, now there's something else I have to do here. Something important. Something true.

"I want to promise you something, Mamma. If I don't ever swim back home, now it won't be because I was too scared. It will be because I found my courageous heart, and did something I knew deep inside was really good to do.

"And if somehow, if somehow I do make it back to the water again, I promise you, Mamma, I will start the Big Swim home as soon as I have the strength. And even though it will be a long, long journey, and I may be scared sometimes, I won't give up, and I won't quit, until I see you and Poptail again.

"I love you, Mamma. I miss you. And if I'm going to get a chance to start swimming home, I need to feel your love in my heart. I need to feel your hope and your support and your strength and your spirit. I need to know you're with me.

"I wish somehow you could know, Mamma. I wish somehow you could know I'm alive. I wish somehow you could know that I'm following my heart, and helping a young penguin who really needs me. So if I don't ever swim back home to you, now it will be because I did something that I knew in my heart was good to do. Even though it really scares me. Puddly gave me the gift of teaching me that. He's helped me find the courage to swim all the way home to you. And if I get the chance, that's what I'm going to do. Dolphin promise. I have to go now, Mamma. I love you."

Far away, on a bright, warm morning, a young dolphin and his mother were swimming in a beautiful blue-green cove, looking up at the morning moon, with Splashers very much in their hearts.

Chapter 24
Focus Forward

Splashers swam back to Puddly, filled with determination and purpose. "Back up a little. I'm going to hop up onto the ice." He lifted the front of his body out of the water, and then with a quick flip of his tail, he lifted himself up onto the ice. Then he scooted forward a little to test things out. "I think I'll be able to do this for a little while, Puddly." He scooted around to face the water, and looked up at the moon. He took in a deep breath of the fresh, salty ocean air, then turned back to Puddly. "I'm ready. Let's get moving."

"Okay, Splashers. If you're sure about this."

"I am, Puddly." Splashers scooted a few scoots to get in front of Puddly, and then kept scooting forward, flattening the snow as he went.

"Hey, you're pretty good at that, Splashers. You doing okay?"

"I'm okay, Puddly. Let's get you home."

"I'm really sorry you're having to do this, Splashers. I really, really am."

"I know you are," Splashers said, breathing heavily. Then he stopped and turned towards Puddly. "We all make mistakes, young penguin. And I know you've learned from yours and your heart is sorry. But feeling bad won't help you get home, Puddly. The best thing you can do for yourself right now is to let your heart really forgive yourself. And then to focus all your attention on what's in front of you. I need you to put all your energy into just getting yourself back home to safety before the Night Winds. Once you're home, you can look back if you want to. But for now, we need to focus forward. Okay, Puddly?"

"Okay, Splashers. I'll do my very best to focus forward until I'm home. Can you see that little hill way ahead? That's Sea Way Hill. We just head straight for that. This would have been a lot harder and slower for me without you smushing down the snow, Splashers. You're the very kindest dolphin I've ever met!"

They started moving forward slowly again, with Splashers leading the way. Before long, he stopped to rest for a few moments.

"You still doing okay, Splashers?"

"Okay," Splashers said. "Just catching... my breath."

"You want me to sing *Steady and Strong*, Splashers? That's the waddle song Papa sang to me two nights ago. And I sang it yesterday when I was too tired to keep waddling. You want to hear it?"

"Okay, Puddly," Splashers said, as he started struggling forward again.

"Great! Here it is.

"Steady and strong
We waddle along
Step after step
Singing this song
We won't give up
And we won't turn around
And we'll get back up
If we ever fall down
And sooner or later
Sure as the sun

We'll get where we're going
And then we'll be done!"

Splashers stopped for a few moments again, to rest and catch his breath. When he started scooting again, he said "I like that, Puddly. Sing it again."

Puddly sang the song a few more times, with Splashers stopping to rest after each time. He needed a little longer to rest with every stop, and he was starting to scoot more slowly.

"You okay, Splashers? You sure are breathing hard."

"I'm... okay... Puddly."

"Hey look, Splashers! Sea Way Hill is a lot closer than it was! And it looks like now that we're farther from the ocean, there's not as much new snow, and it isn't quite as deep! Maybe I can make it from here on my own!"

Splashers stopped again and looked at Sea Way Hill off in the distance in front of him. Then he looked back behind him at Puddly, and at the long trail of flattened snow that disappeared into the vast white emptiness now between him and the ocean. Then he looked up at the moon for a few moments. As he turned back around, he said quietly to himself, "Focus forward. Focus forward."

"What is it, Splashers? Do you need to go back now? It's okay if you do. I think I can make it from here. You've already saved me from having to push through a whole lot of snow. And you've been breathing harder and moving slower and I know this is really really hard for you. Maybe you should go back now to make sure you have enough energy."

"Don't worry about that, Puddly. Let's keep getting you closer to home."

"You sure, Splashers?"

"Sure as snow, Puddly."

"Well, if you say so. But you be sure to turn around just as soon as you need to. Okay, Splashers?"

"Just focus forward, Puddly… Focus forward."

Chapter 25
Whole Hearted

Slowly and steadily they got closer and closer to Sea Way Hill. Puddly sang *Steady and Strong* in between rests, and Splashers scooted along in rhythm to the words, slower than before.

"Steady and strong
We waddle along
Step after step
Singing this song
We won't give up
And we won't turn around
And we'll get back up
If we ever fall down
And sooner or later
Sure as the sun
We'll get where we're going
And then we'll be done!

"Hey look, Splashers! We're getting really close to Sea Way Hill! And from the front of it I'll be able to see Sunshine Hill! And home is right on the other side of it! I know I can make it from here, Splashers! I know I can! And I don't want you to go one scoot farther away from the ocean. Not one!"

"I told you… I would go… as far as I can," Splashers said, breathing heavily. "And I can still go… a little farther."

Puddly waddled in front of Splashers and turned around. "No, Splashers. You're getting slower and tireder and breathing heavier with every scoot. You need to go back now."

"Listen, Puddly," Splashers said weakly. "I feel certain, in my heart, it's my role to go as far as I possibly can. To help make sure you get back home. There could still be some deep snow drifts that could slow you down. I'm not stopping yet, Puddly. I can still go a little more."

"No, YOU listen, Splashers!" Puddly said, filled with determination. "You saved my life last night. And now today you've smushed down the snow all this way for me. I don't know if I could have even made it to Sea Way Hill before dark without your help. But thanks to you, I'm almost there! I know I can make it home from here, Splashers. I'm sure of it! The snow isn't as deep now, and even if I go a little slower in places because of it, thanks to you I still have enough time and energy to get back to Penguin Valley before dark. I'll just keep waddling along, steady and strong, and I'll make it! Sure as snow! I KNOW I can make it, Splashers. And I just don't feel good about you going one scoot farther. Not even one! So I'm not gonna take one more step until you agree to turn around! Not one!"

Puddly plopped down on the snow in front of Splashers. "Believe me, Splashers. I'm just gonna sit right here on my butt until you agree to go back! Penguin promise! And that's the next best thing to a dolphin promise there is!"

Splashers looked at the young penguin in front of him and saw that he meant it. There would be no changing his mind on this one. The best way to make sure Puddly got home before the Night Winds was to let him go alone.

"Okay, Puddly," Splashers said, still breathing heavily. "You win. If the only way to get you waddling home again is for me to stop scooting along with you, I'll stop now."

"That's really great, Splashers!" Puddly said, hopping up to his feet. "I really didn't feel good about you going one scoot farther away from the ocean. Not one. I know this has been awfully hard for you. It's the nicest thing anyone has ever done for me ever! But you need to get back to the water where you belong. Then you can go home to your mamma and brother. You sure you can make it back, Splashers? I can tell you're really, really tired."

Splashers looked away. "Don't worry about me, young penguin. But I think I'm going to just rest here a little while first. We dolphins, once we rest a while, we get a second wave of energy and there's no stopping us. Now get going, my young friend. Your family is worried about you."

"Awwwe, Splashers. Then this means goodbye. This means I won't ever see you again."

"Look up at the moon, Puddly. Sometimes when you look at it, you'll think of me. And we'll always be connected."

"And sometimes when you look at the moon, you'll think of me too. Right, Splashers? And maybe sometimes we'll both be looking at it at the exact same time! Awwwe. I'm gonna miss you, Splashers. I really really am. I'm not very good at goodbyes yet. Because this is my very first one."

Puddly waddled up closer and leaned his forehead against Splashers' head. Then he looked up at the moon, trying not to cry. "I really don't want to leave you, Splashers. But you scooted all this way to help me get home before dark, and I know that's what I have to do."

"Remember, Puddly. On your way home, it's okay have some sadness in your heart that we won't see each other again. But you need to focus all your energy on just getting home. It's harder to move forward when your heart is looking backward. So be right where you are, and let all your attention focus forward. Okay, Puddly? Focus forward."

"Okay, Splashers. I promise. I'll focus forward until I'm home safe. Hey, Splashers? Can I tell you something? I know we haven't known each other for very long, but you're my very best friend. Even if you weren't my only real friend, you'd still be my very best one. I'm really gonna miss you, Splashers. I'll never, ever forget you."

"I'll miss you too, Puddly." Splashers gathered all the energy he had left to say, as strongly as he could, "Go on home now, young penguin. Go on home."

"I will, Splashers. Right now. You get home too, okay? You start scooting back to the ocean really soon. And then after you rest up, you get back home to your mamma and Poptail, okay? Goodbye, Splashers. Goodbye!"

And then, Puddly turned around and started waddling the short distance to Sea Way Hill, and then along its side. He wanted to look back and wave one last time, but he knew he had to put all his energy into getting home, and he was afraid if he looked back at Splashers, half his heart would want him to turn around and waddle back to him. "I don't want half my heart looking backwards right now. I need to get home whole heartedly. Focus forward, Puddly."

Once Puddly knew he had gone around enough of Sea Way Hill that he wouldn't be able to see Splashers if he looked back, he stopped and turned around. He looked for the moon, but it was getting lower, and was hidden behind the hill. "Well, even if I can't see the moon, I can still feel you in my heart, Splashers." Puddly took in a big breath and let it go. "Goodbye, Splashers. I'm really sad I won't ever see you again. But you'll always be right here in my heart. We'll be forever connected." Then he turned back around to start waddling again. "Come on, feet! You can do it! Focus forward!"

Chapter 26
Reunion

Puddly waddled slowly along the side of Sea Way Hill. He had been through so much since the morning before, which felt like forever ago. He was sad to leave Splashers, and each step felt heavy and slow. But he had promised to focus all his energy on waddling home. And he knew once he reached the front of Sea Way Hill, he would be able to see his very own hill waiting for him. "I know you're tired, Puddly. But you just gotta keep moving. You can do it, feet!" He started singing *Steady and Strong* to see if that helped him have more energy. As he sang, he started to feel it in him. He sang it louder and louder, and let it fill him with energy and determination.

"Steady and strong!
I waddle along!
Step after step!

Singing this song!
I won't give up!
And I won't turn around!
And I'll get back up!
If I ever fall down!
And sooner or later!
Sure as the sun!
I'll get where I'm going!
And then I'll be done!"

Puddly's legs were tired, but he knew that thanks to Splashers helping him get through all the deep snow, he would now be able to make it all the way to Penguin Valley before dark. "Awwwe, I miss you, Splashers," he said quietly. But he was also starting to feel home pulling him forward. "I guess it's easier to go back home than to leave. Maybe whatever way you're trying to go, home always pulls you towards it."

Puddly was getting close to the front of Sea Way Hill. "I'll see Sunshine Hill soon! As long as I just take one step at a time, I'm gonna make it! Maybe I'll even find Papa and the fishing group out looking for me! Maybe they'll be calling me!"

He could hear his papa's voice calling him in his mind. "Puddly? Puddly? Where are you? PUDDLY?"

"Wow, my mind sure can make it sound like Papa's really calling me! Hey, wait a blink!" He stopped waddling and listened as hard as he could.

"Puddly? Puddly? Where are you? PUDDLY?"

And suddenly he realized it really WAS his papa calling him! From somewhere just up ahead, in front of Sea Way Hill!

"Puddly? PUDDLY, where are you?"

"Papa! I'm here! I'm here!" Puddly started waddling full speed towards his papa's voice. "I'm here, Papa! Where are you?"

Just then, Puddly made it to the front of Sea Way Hill, and saw his papa coming towards him.

"Papa!"

"Puddly! Puddly, you're okay! You're okay!"

His papa waddled up to him and put his forehead against Puddly's. Then he looked him over to make sure he really was okay. "Puddly! I found you! You're okay?"

"I'm okay, Papa! I really am! I'm so sorry, Papa. I know I messed up so bad. I was just really mad and I just didn't stop to think and my feet just started waddling down Sunshine Hill and I was stupid enough to follow them but Splashers made me admit it was really me that did it, not my feet, and that I wasn't really stupid, I was just stubborn and wanted to have my own way, and I didn't know it was so far to the ocean and I was calling for you yesterday here at Sea Way Hill but it was so windy you couldn't hear me and I tried to keep up with you but I just couldn't, I just couldn't at all, and I didn't know where you were and the wind was so strong and the blowing snow was so bad that I could hardly see and I didn't know what to do so I just kept waddling forward hoping I would find you, and I fell on my butt a few times and once I was so tired I just wanted to lie there in the cold and sleep but I thought of your waddle song, *Steady and Strong*, and I sang it and sang it and sang it and I didn't give up and I finally made it to the ocean but it was starting to get dark and I still couldn't find you and I was so scared and I just didn't see how I was gonna make it until morning because it was already awfully cold and windy, but then Splashers saved me and helped me make it through the night and he even helped me waddle almost all the way here by smushing down the snow, and Mamma must be so worried about me and I know I'm in the biggest trouble any young penguin has ever been in ever but I don't care as long as I'm home with you and Mamma and Nightsong and Fuzzly and you aren't really mean and I do like you and I'm really sorry I messed up so bad and— " Puddly stopped and took in a big breath of the cool, crisp air. "I love you, Papa. And I'm really so very from my heart sorry."

His papa had tears in his eyes. "I love you too, Puddly. I didn't give up hope this morning when I found out you were missing. But I just couldn't imagine how you could have survived last night, out in the Great Open. The Night Winds have been getting worse, but last night was the worst night I can remember. It was so cold we had to leave the ocean and came back here to Sea Way Hill where there was less wind. We all huddled together and it was still a rough night for us."

"But how did you find out I was gone, Papa?"

"When we were halfway home this morning, a few penguins looking for you met us. Everyone's been looking for you, Puddly. Your mamma is so worried about you."

"I know, Papa," Puddly sniffled. "I really do know."

"Puddly Sunfacer Furfoot, don't you EVER do that again! I really didn't know if I would ever see you again!"

"I won't, Papa. I really really won't. Not ever!" Puddly felt the sun on his face a moment. Then he turned away from it. "I really messed up so bad, Papa. I just don't think I deserve to feel the sun on my face for a long long time. I caused everyone so much trouble and worry. I bet right now there's not one penguin in the whole world who still likes me. Not even me."

"I know how you feel, Puddly," his papa said gently. "When I was about your age, I got myself into my own big mess once. And no one was harder on me about it than I was. Then my papa came up to me and said something I won't ever forget."

"What did he say, Papa?"

"He said that every single one of us, over our whole lives, will make as many mistakes as there are snowflakes in a storm. Mostly small ones. Sometimes big ones. And when we close our heart to ourselves after a big mistake, that just makes it a hundred times worse. And when we open our heart to ourselves after a big mistake, that can make it a hundred times better. Sometimes even better than if we hadn't messed up at all. The harder we are on ourselves, the heavier we feel, and the harder it is for us to step forward, make things right as best we can, and then waddle on, with a smile back in our heart. Does that make sense to you, Puddly?"

"I think it makes sense, Papa. It's just kind of hard to like myself very much right now."

"That's how I felt too, at first. Puddly, you're mamma and I love you very much. That love isn't something you ever have to earn. And it isn't something you can ever lose by making a big mistake. It's just something that will always be in our hearts. On your very best days, and on your very worst. Sure as snow. And as you get older, it will more and more be your job to love yourself as much as we love you. On your very best days, and on your very worst. And the best way to be able to give yourself that gift later is to practice giving yourself that gift now. One of the kindest gifts we can ever give ourselves is a warm, open heart when we make a big mistake. That's one of the main things our hearts are for, Puddly. For loving ourselves when we feel like we least deserve it."

Puddly looked at his papa's gentle smile. Then he slowly turned back towards the sun, closed his eyes, and let himself feel the warm sunshine on his face again. He felt it melt a frozen tear on his cheek, that rolled down his face and disappeared into the snow. He took in a big breath of sunshine, and then turned back to his papa.

"I understand, Papa. I really can still be loved by you, by Mamma, by the warm sun, and even by my own heart. Even when I mess up worse than I ever ever have. That feels really good to hear, Papa. I think maybe Splashers was kind of trying to tell me that too. But it's really nice to hear you say it, Papa. It's just really nice to hear you say it."

Chapter 27
Not Much Time

"Puddly, we don't have that much extra time if we're going to get back to Penguin Valley before dark," his papa said. "But before we go, I want to understand a little more about Splashers. Who was he? You said he found you at the ocean and somehow helped you make it through the worst Night Winds I can remember. And then today he came with you almost all the way here?"

"Right, Papa. Yesterday, after I couldn't catch up with you here, the snow was blowing too hard to see Sunshine Hill, so I was just trying to follow you and catch up with you so I could be safe. But I couldn't find you. I was so tired and scared, Papa. I got to the ocean, just barely, but I didn't see you, and it was getting dark and I was just too tired to look for you anymore. But I kept calling and calling for help, even though I just wanted to give up, and Splashers heard me and he saved my life!"

"Tell me who Splashers is, Puddly."

"He's a dolphin, Papa!"

"A dolphin?"

"Right, Papa. They're kind of like big fish, but they aren't a fish at all, and I got the feeling they probably don't really appreciate it very much if you call them a fish. But he was really really nice, and he saved my life! Twice! When it was getting dark and really cold and windy last night, he had me get in the water where I wouldn't be as cold because it's not as windy, and because of my penguin padding. I really really didn't want to because I was so scared. Have you seen how big the ocean is? It's really really big! But he told me I was made to swim and that I really could do it, so after a bunch of tries I finally got in, and you know what? I could swim! I really could! And I floated there and talked with him all night long. The whole night! Except he let me rest on his flipper and I fell asleep until the sun came up. And then this morning, he actually got out of the water and scooted in front of me to smush down all the snow so I could waddle easier! He scooted almost all the way here to Sea Way Hill for me, Papa! Even though it was awfully hard for him. Without him doing that, I don't think I could have even gotten this far before dark!"

"Puddly, a sea creature flattened down the snow for you almost all the way here?"

"He really did, Papa! For real!"

"And he didn't have legs?"

"No, Papa. He just scooted in front of me the whole way! He had to stop and rest a lot, and he was getting really really tired, but he did it. And finally, when we had almost made it here to Sea Way Hill and I knew I could make it the rest of the way home, I told him I wouldn't go one step more, not even one, until he stopped, so he did. He said he needed to rest a while, but right after that he was gonna start scooting right back to the ocean. What is it, Papa? You look kind of worried."

"Puddly, penguins are very special because we're made for the sea and the ice. But sea creatures can't move around much on ice at all. That's why we never see them around here. But this dolphin not only saved your life last night, he also somehow scooted all that way for you today too. And it seems to me the very least we can do is go back to where you left him and just make sure he's getting back to the ocean okay."

"Sure, Papa! He's probably already scooted pretty far, so we might not even be able to see him at all. But we can try! Maybe I'll get to see Splashers again after all! Even if it's just from a distance! He was just on the other side of Sea Way Hill, Papa. Come on, I'll show you!"

As they waddled around Sea Way Hill, Puddly told his papa more about what had happened since he left Penguin Valley.

"Puddly, we're very, very lucky Splashers was nearby and heard you and came to help you. Without him, I don't see how you would have gotten through the night."

"I know, Papa! Splashers is the greatest dolphin ever! We're almost there! I'll show you where we said goodbye!"

As they reached the back of Sea Way Hill, they saw Splashers, ahead of them in the snow. He was still lying where he was before. He wasn't moving. And his eyes were closed.

Chapter 28
Nothing Left

Puddly waddled up to Splashers as fast as he could, with his papa close behind. "Wake up, Splashers! My papa found me! He's here! I'm safe! We did it! But why are you still here?"

Splashers didn't move.

"Are you sleeping, Splashers? Wake up. Wake up, Splashers. Are you okay?"

Splashers still didn't move.

"Splashers? Splashers, wake up! You have to wake up, Splashers! You just have to! You have to! Please, Splashers. Wake up!"

Slowly, Splashers began to open his eyes. They didn't have the same light and life and heart and power that Puddly was used to.

"You okay, Splashers? You okay?"

"Hey Puddly," Splashers said weakly. "What do you call a dolphin that's just lying in the snow in the middle of nowhere?"

Puddly smiled. "I don't know, Splashers. What?"

"Still Splashers."

"Papa, this is Splashers! He saved my life! Splashers, this is my papa!"

"Puddly told me what you did for him, Splashers. Without you, he wouldn't have made it. We're forever, forever grateful."

"But Splashers," Puddly said. "Why haven't you started back yet? You gotta get back to the water! You just got to!"

"Just need to rest now, Puddly. Just need to sleep."

"You sound so tired, Splashers. You don't sound good at all."

"Don't worry about me, Puddly. Go on home now."

"But Splashers—"

"Go on home, Puddly. Just need to sleep."

"You're not gonna even TRY to go back to the ocean, are you, Splashers? You weren't EVER planning to make it back, were you? You weren't EVER planning to save enough energy to make it back to the water so you could swim home!"

"What mattered was helping you be safe, Puddly. And now you are."

"But I still don't understand, Splashers. Why was that what mattered most? Why was that worth giving up ever being in the ocean again? Ever being with your Mamma and Poptail again? Why was that worth giving up everything, Splashers? Why?"

"I just knew it in my heart, Puddly. And that's the only why a dolphin ever needs."

"But you said you'd be okay, Splashers! You told me you could get back!"

"I'm sorry, Puddly. I was trying to save your life. It's really okay. I helped save a very special young penguin. You're with your papa now. You're safe. Now go on home."

Splashers looked at the moon, low in the sky. "Mamma. Poptail. Think of me when you look at the moon. And we'll always be connected."

Puddly wiped a tear sickle from his cheek. "You have to promise me you won't give up, Splashers! You just have to! Dolphin promise me!"

Splashers closed his eyes.

"Dolphin promise me, Splashers!"

"I'm sorry, Puddly," Splashers said quietly, with his eyes still closed. I didn't want you to find out. I just don't have anything left in me. It's really okay. You need to go on home to your mamma now."

"But Splashers—"

"Nothing left to say, Puddly. Just nothing left. Let me sleep now."

"No, Splashers! No! We have to save him, Papa! We HAVE to! He saved my life! He scooted all the way here for me! And he always knew he probably wasn't ever gonna make it back to the ocean! I can't believe he did that for me, Papa! He just can't die! He just can't! We HAVE to help him get back to the water, Papa! We just have to!"

"I just don't know what we can do, Puddly," his papa said. "He's just too big for us to move him. If he's going to make it back to the water, he's going to have to find the strength inside himself. Maybe you can help him find that, Puddly. I honestly don't know."

Just then, two penguins from the fishing group, Stumbles and Blizz, came waddling up. "You found him! You found Puddly!"

"I'm really sorry for all the trouble I caused," Puddly said. Then he looked at Splashers. "So very sorry."

"This dolphin saved Puddly's life," his papa said. "Now he needs to get back to the ocean. But he's exhausted, and he's given up. And if we leave now, he won't even try. Puddly and I are going to stay with him and try to help. That means we might only be able to get as far as Sea Way Hill before dark, and even if we're mostly out of the wind, it's going to be too cold for just the two of us."

"Don't worry," Stumbles said. "We'll go tell the rest of the fishing group you found Puddly, and we'll all meet you at Sea Way Hill at sunset so we can huddle together tonight."

"Papa, do you think someone could go back to Penguin Valley and tell Mamma I'm okay? I know she's awfully worried."

"That's a good idea, Puddly. She needs to know, and so does everyone else who's looking for you. Blizz, would you mind going back and spreading the word?"

"I'm on my way!" Blizz said. Then he looked at Splashers. "That's the kindest thing I've ever heard of anyone doing. You rest a little and then you get yourself back into the water where you belong." And with that, he and Stumbles waddled off at full speed towards Sea Way Hill.

Chapter 29
Steady and Strong

As soon as Stumbles and Blizz left, Puddly put all his attention back on Splashers. "You open your eyes right now, Splashers! You open your eyes and look at me! I want to say something to you and I want to know you're listening! I know you can open your eyes again, Splashers. Open them right now! Come on. Open them!"

Splashers slowly opened his eyes.

"Remember earlier, Splashers? You were gonna scoot even farther to make sure I was safe. You wanted to keep going, and I stopped you. That means you DO have some more scoots in you! You don't have to feel like you have enough scoots to make it back to the water right now. All you need to do is turn around to face the ocean and just do one little scoot! That's all you need to find inside yourself right now, Splashers. I know you have one more scoot in you, and you know it too. My life was worth more scoots, but yours isn't even worth one more? The hope of seeing your mamma and Poptail again isn't worth even one more scoot? Look at the moon, Splashers. Look at it!"

Splashers turned his head and looked at the moon.

"See it, Splashers? It's going to be setting soon, but right now it's big and bright and beautiful, and maybe your mamma and Poptail are looking at it right now too! Maybe they're thinking of you and sending you their love through the moon right now, Splashers. Can you feel them? You can see them again, Splashers! You really can! All you have to do right now is just turn yourself around and move forward just one scoot! I know you can do that much, Splashers! I know you have it in you! Just turn around and move one little scoot forward! You can do it, Splashers! You really, really can! Just turn around and scoot one scoot! Just one little scoot!"

Splashers slowly looked back at Puddly. "You aren't going to stop talking until I do, are you, young penguin?"

"Nope! I'm just gonna get louder and louder and talk faster and faster and keep you from any peace and quiet at all! So you might as well get your dolphin butt turned around and give me just one scoot! I know you have it in you, Splashers! Just one scoot! You can do it! Come on!"

Splashers looked back at the moon a moment, took a few big breaths, wiggled his body a little to wake it up, and slowly turned around.

"That's the way, Splashers! I knew you could do it! I knew it! Now just one little scoot! Just one! I know you have one scoot inside you, ready to come out. You had some more for me, so I know you can find one more scoot for you. You can do it, Splashers! Just one little scoot!"

Splashers took in a big breath, gathered his strength, and scooted forward one scoot. Then he closed his eyes again.

"That's it, Splashers! That's the way! See? I knew you had it in you! I knew you could do it! And you know you have another scoot in you, Splashers. That's all you have to find inside yourself right now. Just the energy for one more scoot. Open your eyes and just do one more scoot, Splashers! Just one more scoot!"

Splashers opened his eyes slowly, wiggled a little more, and scooted again.

"That's the way, Splashers! I knew you could do it! I knew you could! Now just imagine swimming up to Poptail, and he's so excited to see you, and you're so glad to be home! Just imagine it, Splashers! Imagine how fast you'll swim up to him once you see him! He'll be swimming to you too, but I bet you'll be swimming to him even faster! You'll be so excited, Splashers! Just imagine it! See it! Feel it! Just do a double scoot for Poptail right now, Splashers! Imagine he's right in front of you and just scoot two scoots right to him! Come on! Just two little scoots!"

Splashers opened his eyes a little wider, and looked a little more awake. He gathered his strength and scooted two more times.

"That's great, Splashers! That's really great! Now, just imagine that after you swim up to Poptail, you see your mamma a little ways in front of you! It will be the happiest moment of her life! See her there, Splashers! Imagine how happy you'll both be as you swim up to her at full speed! How about three scoots towards her, Splashers? I know you have it in you! Just focus forward! Just feel home pulling you towards it! Home does that! It pulls you towards it! Just three scoots towards home, Splashers! Three scoots towards your mamma! You can do it! Just three scoots!"

Splashers took in a big breath, looked at the moon again, wiggled his tail, and scooted forward three more times.

"You're doing it, Splashers! You're really doing it!! The ocean is getting closer with every scoot! You're gonna make it, Splashers! Just imagine how great it will feel to be back home! To see your family and friends and the beautiful coral reef. You can be there again, Splashers! You can be back home with your mamma and Poptail again! You really can. Scoot another scoot, Splashers! Scoot another scoot!"

Splashers scooted again. And again.

"That's it, Splashers! That's it! I think maybe I can see the ocean not too far ahead! And when you get there, you can rest all you want! And then when you're all rested up, you can start the swim home! And it's gonna go faster than you think, and before you know it, you'll be home again! You really will, Splashers! You'll be home! Scoot again, Splashers! Scoot again!"

Splashers gathered his strength and scooted a few more times.

"That's the way! You're gonna make it, Splashers! You really are! Sure as snow! Sure as the warm beautiful blue green waters where your mamma and Poptail and all your friends are waiting for you! You really can do it, Splashers! You really can!"

Splashers looked at Puddly. "Just maybe… you're right," he said weakly. "Just maybe… I can."

"I KNOW you can, Splashers! I KNOW you can! You know if getting to the ocean was the only way to save my life, you would do all you could to get there! You know you would, Splashers! Well saving your own life is worth just as much effort! But right now, all you need to find in you is just this next scoot. That's all! I believe in you, Splashers! Just this next scoot is all you have to make happen right now. Just this next scoot!"

And bit by bit, Splashers slowly scooted closer and closer to the ocean, with Puddly helping him find the strength, again and again, to scoot just a little more.

"Hey! I can see the ocean up ahead, Splashers! I really really can!"

"I thought… you said… you saw it before," Splashers said, breathing heavily.

"Well, maybe earlier I kind of stretched the truth just a little. But I really do see it now, Splashers! Penguin promise! It's really not that much farther! We're gonna make it, Splashers! We really are! Look at the moon again! It's just starting to set. Maybe your mamma and Poptail are looking at it right now too, sending you heart ripples! Just keep imagining swimming to them, Splashers! They'll be so happy to see you! You'll be able to tell them everything that's happened! And how you saved my life! Twice! Your mamma will be so proud of you, Splashers! She really, really will!

"Steady and strong!
We scoot along!
Scoot after scoot!
Singing this song!"

Splashers started scooting in rhythm to Puddly's words.

"We won't give up!
And we won't turn around!
And we'll get back up!
If we ever fall down!
And sooner or later!
Sure as the sun!
We'll get to the ocean!
And then we'll be done!

"That's the way, Splashers! That's the way!" Puddly turned to his papa. "He's gonna make it, Papa! He really really is!"

"I think you're right, Puddly!" his papa said. "Thanks to you, I really think you're right!"

"Hey listen, Splashers!" Puddly said. "The ocean! I can hear it! I really can! We're almost there! You're almost in the water again! In just a few more scoots it will just be a few more scoots until it's only a few more scoots! You're gonna make it, Splashers! Steady and strong! Steady and strong! You're really gonna make it!"

Splashers saw the ocean not too far in front of him, and then he started to hear it. "I think... I think I'm going to make it, Puddly. I think I'm going to make it!" He started scooting faster.

"You're really gonna do it, Splashers! You really really are! You're almost there! I know you can do it, Splashers! Just focus forward! Just a few more last scoots! That's all! Just a few more last scoots!"

Splashers got a burst of energy and kept scooting and scooting right up to the edge of the ice. Then, just as the moon disappeared below the horizon, with one last big scoot, he splashed into the water. Splashers had made it.

Chapter 30
Forever Connected

Puddly waddled up to the edge of the ice, excitedly. "You made it, Splashers! You made it! I knew you could do it, I just knew it! You're gonna be okay! He's gonna be okay, Papa! He really is! If you hadn't found me, Papa, and if you hadn't wanted to go back and check on him, Splashers never would have made it back ever! Thank you, Papa!"

"You saved his life, Puddly," his papa said, proudly. "One scoot at a time, you saved his life."

"That idea came from your song, Papa! I just KNEW Splashers had it in him! I just knew it! Splashers, you really made it! You really really did! You're gonna be okay now, right, Splashers? You're gonna be okay?"

Splashers was swimming around slowly, feeling how good it was to be back in the water again.

"Yes, I'm going to be okay now, Puddly. Thanks to you. I'll probably be a little weak for a few days, but soon I'll be as good as new. And even better, because now I know that having a courageous heart doesn't mean not being scared. It's doing what I know is good to do, even if it really scares me. You taught me that, Puddly. If you hadn't come along, I really don't know if I ever would have started the Big Swim at all. But thanks to you, I'm going to start it tomorrow. Even if I'm a little slow for a few days. And even if I feel scared sometimes."

"Really, Splashers? You really are?"

"Dolphin promise!"

"That's great, Splashers! That's really really great!"

Puddly's papa stepped up to the edge of the ice. "Thank you again, Splashers, for all you did for Puddly. We'll always be deeply grateful, and we'll never forget you."

"And thank you both," Splashers said, "For not giving up on me. When I already had."

"I guess that's why there are friends, Splashers," Puddly said. "because no one can hold themselves up all the time. That would just be too tiring."

Puddly's papa looked at the sky. "We need to be heading back now, Puddly. We have to get back to Sea Way Hill before the Night Winds. Do you think you can waddle all the way there again?"

"Can we sing *Steady and Strong* to help me, Papa?"

"Sure we can, Puddly!"

"Then I can do it, Papa! I've walked more yesterday and today than in my whole life put together, but I can make it! One step at a time, I can make it!"

Then Puddly looked at Splashers, in front of him in the water. "Awwwe, I don't want to leave you, Splashers. This really is saying goodbye forever. I'm really really gonna miss you." Puddly jumped into the water and swam up to him. He leaned his forehead against Splashers' for a moment. "I'll think of you every time I see the moon, Splashers. Every time. And we'll be forever connected."

"I'll think of you too, Puddly," Splashers said. "And we'll be forever connected." Then he lifted Puddly back onto the ice with his tail. "Goodbye, young penguin."

"Goodbye, Splashers! I'll never, ever forget you! Penguin promise!" Puddly wiped away a tear sickle, made his feet turn around, and focused forward, as he started waddling back towards Sea Way Hill with his papa.

~ ~ ~ ~ ~

It was almost dark when Puddly and his papa reached the fishing group waiting for them at Sea Way Hill. As they all huddled together to stay warm, away from the worst of the wind, Puddly stayed right next to his papa. As tired as he was, for much of the night he watched the sky, trying to catch the stars moving, and waiting for the moon to rise. When it finally started to come up, he watched it slowly lift itself into the sky, almost as big and bright as the night before. And he had a strong feeling that at that very moment, Splashers was looking at it too. "And that same moon is shining down on Mamma. And Nightsong. And Fuzzly. And Splashers' mamma. And his brother, Poptail."

As Puddly watched the moon slowly climb higher into the sky, he thought of Splashers on his Big Swim back home to his family. And somehow, he knew in his heart, sure as snow, that Splashers would make it home safe and happy, and sooner than he imagined. And Puddly thought of tomorrow, when he would be back home with his whole family in Penguin Valley. "Awwwe, I'll get to feel the sun on my face again on Sunshine Hill. That's about as far away from home as I want to go by myself for a long, long time."

And as Puddly's eyes grew heavy, and he started to drift off, he noticed that even though it was bitter cold, his heart felt as soft and warm and happy as whenever the morning sun warmed his face. He leaned against his papa, took a deep, contented breath, and let the warmth in his heart spread all through him. Then he drifted off into the land of dreams, where he swam with Splashers, under the bright, beautiful dolphin moon, joining him on his Big Swim back home.

About the Author

Bryant Oden is best known for his funny Songdrops songs, which have frequented iTunes charts around the world, and have over 250 million views on YouTube. His songs, including *Best Friends Forever, I Got a Pea*, *The Tarantula Song*, *Before I Could Rhyme*, *The CBA Song*, and dozens more, have found an audience in all age groups, from toddlers to teens and beyond. The viral sensation, *The Duck Song*, has over 130 million YouTube views. For more information about Bryant Oden, please visit Songdrops.com or Puddly.com.

Illustrations by Brian Warner
Book design by Miguel S. Kilantang Jr.

Made in the USA
Lexington, KY
23 April 2013